WHAT WE'RE SCARED OF

KEREN DAVID

SCHOLASTIC

Published in the UK by Scholastic Children's Books, 2020
Euston House, 24 Eversholt Street, London, NW1 1DB, UK
A division of Scholastic Limited.

London – New York – Toronto – Sydney – Auckland
Mexico City – New Delhi – Hong Kong

SCHOLASTIC and associated logos are trademarks and/or
registered trademarks of Scholastic Inc.

Text © Keren David, 2021
Chapters 43 and 44 © Mala Tribich MBE, Reproduced
with permission of Mala Tribich MBE

The right of Keren David to be identified
as the author of this work has been asserted by her
under the Copyright, Designs and Patents Act 1988.

ISBN 978 1407 19644 2

A CIP catalogue record for this book
is available from the British Library.

Printed by CPI Group (UK) Ltd, Croydon, CR0 4YY
Papers used by Scholastic Children's Books are made
from wood grown in sustainable forests.

1 3 5 7 9 10 8 6 4 2

This is a work of fiction. Names, characters, places, incidents
and dialogues are products of the author's imagination or are used
fictitiously. Any resemblance to actual people, living or dead,
events or locales is entirely coincidental.

www.scholastic.co.uk

For my parents, Shirley and Joseph, who handed on my Jewish heritage with so much love and care.

Every person in this book is fictional, except one. Every word of Mala Tribich's testimony is true.

"What have I in common with Jews? I have hardly anything in common with myself and should stand very quietly in a corner, content that I can breathe."

Franz Kafka

Our story is just one small part of a much longer one. A story of hate and fear, violence and flight that stretches back hundreds of years.

We thought we were safe and free. We thought the hate was over. We thought it would never happen again. We didn't pay attention. We thought we were safe. We didn't even realize we were part of this story.

We didn't know there was anything to be scared of.

Were we wrong?

CHAPTER ONE

EVIE

There are a hundred pairs of eyes watching me. My stomach is churning like a washing machine; sweat tickles my back. What am I scared of? I only have to make them laugh.

I step up to the mike.

"So, hello everyone. I'm Evie. I'm one half of the world's least identical set of twins."

Beat. Silence, apart from a loud bark of laughter which I know comes from my best friend, Amina. It's too much, too little, too early and too late all at once. Comedy is all about timing, I know that much. My mouth feels dry.

"My twin is six foot tall, slender, elegant and blonde. I'm … not made like that."

It's cheap to invite people to laugh at my body – five foot one and curves like a Kardashian – but I'm used to it. And it works. A ripple of giggles runs through the audience. It's like meat to a starving dog. And that dog is me.

"Our parents were worried that we'd lose our identities if we were brought up with the same clothes and friends and stuff," I go on. "They didn't want us to be confused. So they sent my sister off to boarding school when she was three and I stayed home. When she came home on our tenth birthday, I couldn't even remember her name. So I guess their plan worked?"

Proper laughter now. Amina's laugh is the loudest, but there are definitely other people joining her.

"We never wore identical clothes. We divided up the colours between us. That's why you'll never see me wearing blue, green or red. Our parents searched for months before they found a school with a uniform that I was allowed to wear.

Shame it was this one, eh?"

A proper laugh now! And it's true; no one would ever choose to wear our uniform, which is a shade of brown that the head teacher calls *chestnut* but – well. Let's just say it resembles something else entirely.

"Meanwhile, my sister goes to St Margaret's, in that place, miles away ... what's it called, you might have been there ... ah yes. North London."

No laugh. I guess it's a bit of a cliché for south London people like us to laugh at north London. I make a mental note to work on that joke.

"They have, like, proper hard subjects there. She's learning Latin and Greek. While here, we get really good at self-defence."

OK – people don't like jokes that put down their school. Good lesson. Bad time to learn it. Now, what comes next?

What?

What?

People are whispering. People are shuffling their feet. I'm losing my audience. "OK, guys, last one."

They're quiet again.

"So… A Muslim, a Christian and a Jew walk into a bar."

Murmurings in the audience. Ms Turnberry, head of drama and comedy competition head judge, frowns. Too late, I remember her strict instructions: *No content that could offend any section of the school community.*

"And the barman says, 'What is this, a joke?'"

I think it's a pretty good punchline, actually. And not offensive at all. But my voice is wavery and weak and the joke doesn't land as it should do. "That's it, I'm Evie Harris, vote for me, good night and thank you!"

I don't know who threw the doughnut at my head. I do know that it gets stuck in my hair. *And* gets the loudest laugh any of us managed that night.

It's when I'm backstage, combing sugar sprinkles out of my frizzy hair, wiping icing off my nose, that Ms Turnberry tells me I'm disqualified.

CHAPTER TWO

LOTTIE

I can't breathe.

I really can't. The other girls in the dance studio are all holding their noses and complaining about the stink of the new paint job – but I can't breathe. My chest is tight, my breath is coming in short gasps, I'm about to start wheezing… It's an asthma attack.

"Settle down, girls," says the supply teacher. "I know the smell's bad, but we'll open all the windows and make the best of it."

I stumble to my feet. "Lottie? Lottie, are you all right?"

It's a girl called Hannah, who sits behind me in maths. We've never even spoken before. My friends, Saffy, Topaz, Melanie, are all too busy squealing and flapping their hands under their noses, hoping to delay the start of class, to notice that anything is wrong.

Hannah grabs my bag and marches me to the door. "Miss! Lottie's having an asthma attack! I'm going to take her outside!"

The supply teacher doesn't know the protocol. She should be the one taking me to the school nurse. "Are you sure?" she wavers, while Hannah picks up my bag, opens the studio door and pushes me gently into the corridor.

"I'll take her to the school nurse," she says firmly.

"I could take her," I hear Saffy say, but we're already outside.

And then we're out in the courtyard and she's guiding me to a bench.

"Is your inhaler in your bag?" she asks. She sounds so calm. No wonder the teacher trusted her.

I can't speak, but I nod and gesture to the outer pocket. But I feel better already in the fresh air. Hannah unzips the pocket, finds the inhaler and hands it to me.

I inhale. My lungs feel like they are bursting, and I worry I haven't taken enough in, but when I count to ten and let my breath out, I find that I can breathe again. Gradually, I stop panicking. This is not the day I'm going to die. The medicine is working. It's all OK.

Hannah is watching me carefully.

"Thanks!" I manage to gasp.

Hannah shakes her head. "Don't worry about it. If I'm honest, it's good practice. I mean, not that I have anything against dance. It's exercise, I suppose. But if you want to be a doctor one day... Well, I'm not going to cure anyone by pretending to be a nymph or a lemon or whatever it is she had in mind for us today. Hey – are you crying?"

I shake my head, no, and try and wipe away the tears. Hannah hands me a tissue and says, "Don't be embarrassed," in a kind but brisk way, as though she spends most days mopping up people's tears.

We sit in silence for a bit. My tears stop. My breathing comes back to normal. At last I can talk.

"I'm sorry," I say. "I feel stupid crying. It's just … it's a bit scary when that happens."

My sister and I were born early – twins often are. We were tiny, tiny babies, and my lungs hadn't developed properly. Over the years I've had to spend a long time in hospitals with chest infections, watching Mum and Dad's worried faces, feeling like every breath could be my last.

As a result I worry about germs, chemicals, pollution. The doctors say my asthma is only mild now, that I can keep it under control so long as I use the inhalers properly. I shouldn't be scared. But it's hard to break the habit of a lifetime.

"I don't think we've ever talked before," says Hannah. "Which is strange, as we're in all the same sets."

Obviously I can't tell her why we haven't spoken. That my friends call her weird and laugh at her short hair and round glasses, and think she's a show-off because last year in English she put Saffy right on a chapter of *Jane Eyre* that Saffy clearly hadn't read. "I know," I say, "it is strange we've never spoken."

As I say it, I despise myself for falling in so quickly with my friends' judgements. When I arrived at the school, I ended up making friends with anyone I could, because I was scared of being alone. I was so relieved when Saffy, Topaz and Melanie included me in their group. But a shared interest in tennis, plus all of us looking alike – tall, fair hair, blue eyes – turned out not to be a great way of meeting my soulmates. We're like a matching set of suitcases from the outside – with completely different contents.

"At least we're talking now," I say, "even if it's a couple of years late."

"Year Nine is the best for getting to know people, my brother told me," she says. She looks at her watch – she's got an old-fashioned one, with a black leather strap. "Ten minutes to go. No point going back. No point going to the school office either, unless you want them to call your parents. Did you do that history essay?"

And so we sit and chat, until the bell rings and the studio door opens and my friends are upon us. "Are you OK?" "Lottie, you genius, you missed the whole thing!" "Sorry you got stuck with that weirdo!"

I look around, worried that Hannah overheard. But she's gone.

We walk together to the dining hall, with Saffy going on and on and about how she should have been the one looking after me, and she would have been if Hannah hadn't grabbed me.

"Honestly, I was just about to, Lottie. But she got there before me."

"They're just so pushy," says Topaz. "Think they own the place."

"Well, you know, they could probably afford to," says Saffy.

Melanie giggles. "I bet most of them paid extra to get a place here."

I'm baffled. Why are they calling Hannah *they*? Is Hannah trans?

But then Topaz says, "All Jewish people, they're all like that. My dad says…" and I get it. And I feel sick, and yet sort of ashamed and embarrassed too. And upset with myself because – to be completely honest – I've heard them say things like this about other groups of people ("those Asian girls", "that Muslim lot") and just tried to ignore it.

I know that I ought to say something. For example: "Jewish people like my mum?"

But I don't.

I'm too scared.

CHAPTER THREE

EVIE

I'm spraying snowflakes with silver paint and Dad's sorting through the Christmas tree decorations which he's just brought down from the attic.

"Here are the gingerbread men you made in Year Four," he says. "Raw talent, even then, Evie. And the fairy for the top of the tree..."

McGonagall, next door's enormous tabby cat, is lying on the radiator. He's not really meant to come into our house, because it might trigger Lottie's asthma, but he's so cute that we can't resist him.

"Are you sure you're not upset about the contest?" says Dad for the millionth time. "Because I can email the school if you want. They had no right to disqualify you."

"Rule 3, subsection b," I say. "No mention of religion, race, nationality, sexuality."

"But your joke wasn't offensive. It was actually quite clever."

Dad doesn't mean to sound patronizing, I am sure. But still.

"I know! It's a good joke! But Ms Turnberry said some Muslim people might be offended because it mentioned going into a bar…"

Dad snorts and I know he's about to say something lame about political correctness and woke-ness. But instead he takes a side swerve into some weird ethnic sideline.

"You could say it draws on your Jewish heritage," he suggests. "It's a riff on a classic joke."

"Dad, I am not Jewish." I roll my eyes. Honestly, he's so keen for me to identify with fifty per cent of my family tree. He's not even Jewish, Mum is, and she isn't bothered. Quite the opposite.

She'd rather forget all about it.

"Actually, according to Jewish law, you are," he says. Eye-roll number two.

"I know, thanks, whatever," I say.

"You shouldn't feel ashamed of your heritage, Evie," says Dad, whose own heritage is 75% English, 20% Irish and 5% Danish, according to the DNA test he took a few years back (a birthday present from his Auntie Vera). I never see him dancing Irish jigs or dressing as a Viking. "You should feel proud," he adds. "Being Jewish is a big deal."

I'm not sure what he thinks I should be proud of or what the big deal actually is. I just know that pretending to be part of a minority group when you're not really in that group would feel completely bogus.

There was a boy in my class last year who was really full-on Jewish. Jacob Hertzl. He wore one of those skull caps and took loads of days off in September. There might have been some teasing, I don't really know, because I didn't have anything to do with him at all.

All I know is that, one day in November, Jacob wasn't there, and there was a ferocious lecture from our head of year in assembly about bullying. Jacob never came back to school.

"There's no point moaning about what happened to me," I tell Dad. "Show business isn't about fairness. It's about luck and talent and being in the right place at the right time. And not offending people."

"Comedy is *all* about offending people," he says, just as Lottie comes through the door. She's looking pale as usual and wrinkles her nose at the smell of the paint. I put the cap on my paint spray and push the window open, letting in a blast of freezing cold air and letting out McGonagall.

"How was school?" asks Dad. His gaze rests on her, fond and protective. People always want to protect Lottie.

"OK, thanks," she says. "I've got a load of homework to get on with."

Lottie is the kind of person who does her homework as soon as she gets home from school.

I'm the kind of person who does it just before first bell.

"There are chocolate chip cookies," I say, holding out the plate temptingly. "Mum made them."

"Maybe later." She's halfway up the stairs already.

Dad and I look at each other. We rarely talk about it, but I know he's worried about how much Lottie is eating – or not eating. "Take her up some of the cookies, will you?" Dad says at last. "And a glass of milk."

"Of course, my Lord." I've been watching a lot of *Downton Abbey* recently.

Dad pours a glass of milk and puts three cookies on a small plate. "Three is too many," I tell him. "She won't eat more than one."

"I'd be happy with that."

"You need to chill. Let her eat what she wants." I take a cookie. "I'll just help you out there." It's delicious, sweet and chewy, and finished much too soon. I take another, so the plate for Lottie just contains one lonely cookie.

"There. She might just eat that one."

"I'd better take it up," he says. "You're not to be trusted around baked goods."

He walks up the stairs. I can hear him knock at Lottie's door. I can't hear exactly what they're saying but I know the gist – she's not hungry, she'll wait till dinner. My parents have not learned the essential rule of successful parenting, which is to let us run our own lives. We're fourteen years old! In some cultures we'd be finished with school and ready for adulthood. Obviously, that wouldn't necessarily be a good thing. But at least it would be a break from the incessant nagging about eating too much (me), eating too little (Lottie), not working hard enough (me), working too hard (Lottie), watching too much TV (me), exercising too much (Lottie)...

I think it's because neither Mum or Dad have a full-time job. Too much time on their hands.

Dad comes downstairs, milk and cookie still intact. But he's persuaded Lottie to come with him. She makes herself a tea. "Dad says you got disqualified for being offensive," she says. "I'm sorry – I know how much work you put into that routine."

"Evie doesn't have to put any work into being offensive," says Dad, laughing at his own joke.

"I know, right? I mean you'd have been offended if you'd been there, Lottie."

"Why would I have been offended?"

"Because I talk about how we're like the world's least identical twins."

"Do you?" She laughs, nervously. "What do you say?"

"Like how I'm small and fat and you're six foot and beautiful."

"I'm not six foot! I'm not even blonde!" she squeaks. So literal, my sister. In fact she's five foot eleven, and her hair is honey brown. She's all limbs and angles and angelic big blue eyes. And she's definitely beautiful.

She checks her phone and freezes. "Evie! Did you put a picture up of you with a doughnut in your hair?"

I beam at her. "On my insta. Two hundred likes and rising."

"Why would you post that?"

So that no one else can.

"I'm in it for the cheap laughs."

"I would never do that," she says.

"I know." I'm rolling my eyes. "You're the clever, hard-working, quiet and serious twin. Also the pretty twin. And the sporty twin. Not to mention the saintly twin. But I, dear sister, am the funny twin, and also the performing twin. That's why I'm doing stand-up and you're at the posh school, top of the Latin class, star of the tennis team and asking for goats for Christmas."

Lottie goes bright pink. But it's all true. She passed the exam to go to Mum's old school and I didn't. It stresses her out loads. That and the fact that the fees are super high. Ever since Dad lost his job in TV production and started driving an Uber, money has been very tight.

As for the goats … well, Saint Lottie wants to help others, rather than get presents for herself. It's either heart-warming or vomit-inducing, depending on how you see it.

"Loads of people have left comments," she

says, looking at my post. "Some of them are OK. Someone called 'Luke123' has said, 'Only you could make a doughnut look good'."

My hand goes into some sort of accidental spasm, and I smash a shiny green bauble. "Oh! Luke … who?"

Surely, surely Luke Braybourne hasn't actually left a comment on my Insta? I didn't know he had an account. I didn't know he had any idea who I was. I didn't think he was the sort to go in for online doughnut-related flirting, but never mind, I'll take it…

"This one?" says Lottie, showing me.

Oh. It's Luke Turner from my science class. He's a total creep. Never mind.

I have a secret crush on Luke Braybourne, of 9B. I haven't even told Amina about it. It's partly because of his cute-but-geeky face, but it's also because of how passionate he is. About important stuff like climate change. Things that I don't really know that much about, but that he makes sound really interesting. He's a member of the debate society. Amina and I went last term – she was really interested because it was about welfare cuts, and her mum runs a food bank. I thought it'd be totally boring, but then Luke spoke. He made this incredibly passionate speech which made the teacher who sits in on it tell him to "calm down and check your facts". I fell instantly in love.

I know he'd never look at me. In fact, as he's super tall, and I'm really short, we'd look ridiculous together. But a girl can dream.

It's time for Dad's shift, and like clockwork he starts searching for his keys. Lottie takes over unwrapping the decorations. I ooh and aah as the old favourites come out – the shiny baubles, the reindeer. No angels or baby Jesus. We have a strictly non-religious Christmas. Dad finds his keys and holds them up triumphantly. "I think I'll just watch another episode of that Netflix thing, before I go out on the road," he says, and heads back into the living room.

See? Too much time on his hands.

As if on cue, Mum comes down the stairs, yawning. She's presenting the late night show on

Radio South, which means she's like Lottie's late, lamented hamster, Mr Fluff, who slept all day and then manically ran on his squeaky wheel all night, making him the world's least interesting pet (although I suppose I shouldn't speak ill of the dead). Mum tries to be around during the day to see us off to school and when we come home, but she's a bit of a zombie. So she has early morning baking sessions and leaves us gifts of cookies.

"How're you getting on with those snowflakes, Evie?" she says. I proudly display my work. "Oh, they look beautiful."

"I've done twenty. Is that enough?"

She grins at me, her eyes crinkling. "You can never have too many snowflakes at Christmas!"

Mum *loves* Christmas – not the religious bits, but all the other traditions and rituals. She loves all the songs about snow and chestnuts and reindeers. She loves decorating the house with snowflakes and tinsel. She loves Christmas dinner and Christmas TV and watching the Queen at three p.m. and even Christmas adverts, which make her cry. She's all about mulled wine, and watching old films and decorating the tree. Just don't mention the Baby J-word.

But this year, Lottie is trying to ruin Christmas.

"Look, Lottie you don't really mean it about no presents, do you?" I say, turning to her. "I mean, vouchers for goats – that's a bit boring. No offence."

Lottie takes a careful sip of her tea. "You can all still have presents," she says awkwardly. "I just – I'd prefer it if you supported charities for me."

"Yeah, and now you're the saintly one, and I look greedy and infantile. As usual," I glower.

"That's not true, Evie," Mum jumps in. "It's absolutely fine for you to have presents! We can't all be…" Her voice trails off.

"Perfect?"

"That's not what I meant at all, and you know it."

"I truly do."

Mum shakes her head. An awkward silence fills the room like the stink of burned toast. In fact, if difficult silences could be measured in grades of burned toast, the smoke alarm would be going off right now, with a fire engine just about to turn up at our door. (I like this idea. Maybe I could work it into a routine.)

Dad reappears. "I'm off."

"Shame that you have to work on a sunny Saturday afternoon," says Mum.

"Maybe I'll get lucky," he says cheerfully. "Maybe my first customer will be a Netflix executive desperate for a new sitcom."

Driving Home is Dad's sitcom. It's about a middle aged guy (like him) with a radio presenter wife (like Mum) and twin daughters (like us), who loses his job and starts driving an Uber (like him again). Every week features a different passenger, played – in Dad's dreams – by a different celebrity. Whenever we suggest – tactfully – that car-based comedy has been done already a million times, Dad says, "That's why it works! Originality is dead! We live in an age of reheated leftovers! Fan fiction and remakes!"

"See you..." Mum pauses. "Tomorrow afternoon? I hate this late show."

"I know," Dad says sympathetically. "You'll get something else soon, though. A daytime slot. Something nice and early."

And then – as though someone, somewhere was listening – her phone rings. It's her agent, Fiona. She picks it up.

"Hi," she says wearily. "Before you ask, no I can't do that fundraiser." Fiona starts talking on the other end and Mum goes silent.

Eventually, she says, "He did *what*?" and then goes out, shutting the door behind her.

"That doesn't sound good," says Lottie.

"Maybe they've decided she's too boring, even for the snooze shift," I say. This was funny in my head, but they both look at me like I've kicked a puppy.

"Don't jump to conclusions," says Dad.

I help myself to another biscuit. I wish I'd never said anything. Now we're all thinking the same thing. What if Mum's contract has been cancelled? We'll have even less money than before. Lottie will have to come to my school. We might have to sell the house…

"At least we'd see a bit more of Mum," says Lottie. Little Miss Positive.

At last! The door opens and Mum comes out. She's looking a bit strange. Her face is pink. Her eyes are wide. She goes over to Dad and throws her arms around him.

"There, there," he says, stroking the top of her head. (Dad is six foot one and Mum is five foot two, which explains why Lottie and I are so mismatched.)

Mum says something into his chest.

"It's OK, Bex," he says soothingly. "Whatever it is. We'll cope. I'll do more hours."

"I could go to Evie's school," says Lottie, in the tiniest whisper.

Mum emerges from Dad's manly chest and I see the manic grin on her face. "No, it's good news! I've got a new job! I'm getting the breakfast show on Metro Radio!"

The breakfast show? *Metro Radio*? We all stare at her. That's a nationwide radio show. Everyone listens to the breakfast show. But it already has a host.

"But that's Billy Martin's show!" says Dad, pointing out the obvious. "Billy the king of banter."

"That's just it," says Mum. "They don't want banter any more. It's too problematic. Billy's made a few remarks recently that have brought in lots of complaints. They want someone to be nice and kind and gentle with the listeners. The Voice of Nice on Metro Radio. And that person is me!"

CHAPTER FOUR

LOTTIE

Nothing scares my sister, but I am scared of everything. I'm scared of failing exams (and there are so many to fail). At the moment it's just school tests, but when I'm sixteen there are important exams which will decide my future. I get stomach cramps just thinking about them.

I'm scared of people laughing at me. Of not having friends. Of not being able to think of the right thing to say. Of being noticed. But then also, of being ignored. And then there are some worries that are so huge that it doesn't feel like I can do anything about them. Climate change. Poverty.

War. The Middle East. Pandemics. Terrorism. Racism.

I think a lot about Anne Frank. She'd be an old lady if she were still alive now. Anne Frank was Jewish, just like Mum's side of our family. Because of that she had to hide away for months and months in a dark attic. Then someone betrayed her family, and they were dragged out of hiding and sent to a concentration camp. They weren't killed immediately – most people were – but Anne and her mother and sister all got ill and died. There must have been germs everywhere. They were too weak to resist.

When I was reading Anne's Diary, Mum could see I was getting upset, so she took it away from me. And she said not to worry, it was a long time ago and far away, and it would never happen here and now.

I don't know how she can be so certain. Particularly not when I think about my friends, Saffy, Topaz and Mel. The way they talk about other people. And especially the way they talk about Hannah.

"Is it her hair or is it her glasses that make her look so masculine?" says Saffy.

We're having lunch right next to the packed lunch table where Hannah is sitting with her friends. She has loads of friends, from different classes and year groups, and they're all talking and laughing, and I can only hope that they can't hear our conversation. I wasn't enjoying my cheese sandwich anyway, and now I can't eat it at all. My mouth is too dry.

"Maybe she thinks she looks like Harry Potter," sneers Mel. And actually Hannah does look a bit like Harry Potter, with her dark floppy hair and her serious gaze and her owlish glasses.

"More like Harry Potterstein," says Saffy, putting on a German accent. "I wonder if she's auditioning for the school play – she'd make a perfect Fagin."

I don't understand. And then I do. Fagin, the villain in *Oliver!* who rubs his hands and sings "You've got to pick a pocket or two" is meant to be Jewish.

Hannah glances over. "I heard that. And so

did all my friends. You were being racist."

"I didn't say anything," says Saffy, looking her most innocent. "Did I, Topaz? Did I, Mel?" They shake their heads. "Did I, Lottie?"

Hannah waits. Saffy's eyes bore into mine. And I want to do the right thing. I want to tell her that it's not OK, that she *was* being racist, that I am Jewish, that I don't want to be her friend any more.

"Hannah, can I come and sit at your table? I don't like the company here."

For a minute I think I've said it out loud. But then Hannah shakes her head and says, "I didn't think you were like that, Lottie," and I realize that my brave words stayed in my head unspoken.

CHAPTER FIVE

EVIE

Oh, God, Luke Braybourne. He's here. In the charity shop, on Christmas Eve. With me.

I mean, not *with* me, obviously. We just happen to be in the same space. He works here. And he's dressed as an elf. Yes, an elf.

He's wearing a little green jacket, and tight green trousers, and an elf hat with a little bobble on the end, and somehow manages to look OK. No, he looks better than OK. He looks good. He's dressed as an elf, but he's still got his dignity.

He's not classically beautiful, Luke; he wouldn't make it into a boy band. He hasn't got glossy hair or high cheekbones or dazzling white teeth. His eyes are a muddy brown and so is his curly hair. He's really tall – definitely over six foot – and his legs are skinny, so he looks a bit flamingo-like. Today he's a green flamingo, thanks to the elf outfit. Or perhaps a beanstalk.

But I don't care about that. I'm much more interested in the way his face looks kind all the time – even when he's just eating his lunch or chatting to his friends. And he's so clever. Anyway, he's dressed as an elf like all the staff here, and he's serving at the till and I'm fourth in the queue. I think I'm going to pass out. Although that's possibly because I've been shopping for hours and my arms, legs and back are aching. Just these final presents to buy (well, OK, the pink lace-up boots are for me) and I can collapse on to a bus home … after queueing, that is. There must be thirty people at the bus stop. I only came into this shop because I got bored waiting. And Luke Braybourne is my reward. Along with the pink boots.

I reach the counter, and drop my load in front

of him. Will he recognize me? Do I even want him to?

"Ten pounds for the boots. Two for the duck…" OK, he doesn't have a clue who I am. "Three pounds for the jigsaw … there might be some pieces missing…"

"Doesn't matter, it's for Auntie Vera; she's eighty-seven and she probably won't ever get that far."

He looks up, startled. "Oh, don't say that."

See, I told you. Kind. His brown eyes are wide.

"I was joking," I explain.

"Oh," he says. He frowns. "I recognize you! You were in the competition…"

"Yeah. That was me. Doughnut girl."

"I thought you were funny. They shouldn't have disqualified you. Free speech is an important principle, although obviously one has to weigh that against the potential offence caused…" I stare at him dreamily.

Behind me in the queue someone coughs, in a way that means "it's Christmas Eve, get a move on". I dig out some money. "Here you go."

He takes my money. "Yeah, you were good. If you ever need anyone to help you rehearse your routines or anything, I'd be happy to help. And you should come back to Debate Club…"

"Thank you! That'd be great!" I am smiling so much that I think my face is going to split in two.

"Are you on Snapchat?"

"Yes! Evie Harris! Anyway, happy Christmas! Great costume. It suits you."

Shut up, Evie! Shut up!

He's blushing, which is the cutest thing ever.

"My mum's the manager, she made everyone wear them…"

"It's good to be green," I say, like the song that Kermit sings. I'm about to break into it but luckily the woman behind me has had enough and practically shoves me out of the way, saving me from my own idiocy.

"Byee," I say, as I stuff my shopping into one of my many canvas bags. "Happy Christmas!"

CHAPTER SIX

LOTTIE

I hate Christmas. Noise and fuss and people.
And it's all so fake. Society wants us spending
money on useless stuff, and eating too much
and pretending we're having fun at the same
time.

The build-up – present-buying, decorations,
noisy adverts on television telling you to spend,
spend, spend, eat, eat, eat – is bad enough. I used
to enjoy decorating the tree, but now I don't even
like that. It's too big, too crowded.

I'd prefer a few twigs – sprayed silver maybe
– with blue fairy lights. Or no lights (a waste

of electricity). Just some holly in a vase. That's enough.

Then there's all the food. Turkey, beetroot Wellington (whatever that is) for the vegans, roast potatoes, red cabbage, Brussels sprouts … on and on and on.

Christmas pudding, Christmas cake, chocolate tart (because lots of people don't like Christmas pudding or Christmas cake), lemon tart (because Mum is sure there's someone who doesn't like chocolate either, but she can't remember who it is), fresh fruit salad ("Because there's always someone on a health kick"), cream, custard, crème fraiche…

No one needs this much food. A few weeks ago, I floated the idea that we make rice and dahl and salad, and donate what we would have spent to charity, but Mum just ruffled my hair and said, "It's a beautiful idea, darling, but Christmas is all about celebrating, not suffering." Then I asked what she was celebrating, she took a big gulp of Prosecco and said "life!" and handed me a bag of potatoes to peel.

When we were little we used to light candles for the Jewish festival of Chanucah. Dad was always the one to organize it. And once Mum made potato pancakes, called latkes, which she said are traditional to eat, and she brought out a wooden painted spinning top called a dreidel, and taught us a game to play with it. It was smaller and quieter than Christmas, but that's what I liked about it. But maybe it was too quiet for Mum. She likes to do things big.

Everyone arrives. Dad's Auntie Vera and her "gentleman friend", Sid. Mum's agent, Fiona, and her girlfriend Marie-Christine. Joan and Don who live next door, McGonagall's real owners. He saunters down the stairs to greet them as they arrive.

Then there's Evie's friend Amina, her little sister and big brother, and her parents. Mum had asked me if there was anyone I wanted to invite, and I said no. I didn't explain why, but it's because I don't want to be friends with Saffy and Topaz and Melanie any more. I tried to speak to Hannah to apologize, but she always seemed to be rushing around, busy. And then it was the holidays. I looked her up on social media, but I wasn't confident enough to message her.

"Happy Christmas!" says Mum, greeting everyone with kisses. She's been like a different woman since she stopped the late show, full of energy. She's not starting at Metro Radio till the new year, so she's spent all her time buying new clothes and having photo shoots, and getting facials and going to the gym. And sleeping. She looks great. It's nicer than when she was tired all the time, but it's also a bit much. Amina's parents are now plastered with her fuschia lipstick.

"Thanks for inviting us," says Amina's mum.

"Oh, Christmas is all about togetherness, and getting to know each other, and sharing, isn't it?" says Mum. "Prosecco? Or I have some elderflower fizz…"

Amina and Evie have disappeared upstairs, presumably so Evie can show off her stash of presents. I am attempting to be helpful and invisible, cutting crosses in the bottoms of the Brussels sprouts. But Auntie Vera and Sid are insisting on talking to me, asking relentless questions. Do I like school? Have I got lots of friends? What presents did I get?

"Three goats," I tell them.

"Goats?" says Auntie Vera, peering out of the window to our tiny back garden. "That's a lovely idea, darling. Who will look after them?"

"Families in Ethiopia. They give twelve pints of nutritious milk a week," I tell her.

"So, you're shipping them out there?" Sid says, puzzled.

"No … it's like a donation to charity," I explain.

"Oh, how wonderful. Goodness. What an idea! And that reminds me." Auntie Vera fishes in her bag and hands over a little present, wrapped in sparkly wrapping paper. "For you, sweetie. It's not a goat, but I hope you'll like it."

I smile and say thank you. I told Mum to tell them I didn't want anything, but someone has clearly ignored instructions.

"Aren't you going to open it?"

I do. It's a pair of earrings – amber and silver, and actually very pretty. If only I had pierced ears.

"They're lovely, thank you," I say. Maybe I can sell them and buy another goat…

"Try them now," says Auntie Vera. "They'll look pretty against that blue top. Brings out your eyes, darling."

My top is grey – my favourite colour – but if she wants to call it blue, that's up to her. "I'm afraid I don't have pierced ears," I say, and she oohs with surprise, and then Sid gives me twenty pounds, and says I must get them done right after Christmas.

And then they wander off, Proseccos in hand, and I overhear Auntie Vera say, "She's such a lovely girl, but my oh my, so serious."

And Sid says, "I prefer the little one, she's cheeky, but you can have a bit of a joke with her."

So that's nice.

I wonder what Hannah's doing for Christmas. It must be strange, filling a whole day when most of the country are celebrating.

My phone pings. It's a text from Saffy. *Happy Crimbo! Did you see my Insta post?*

I take a look. Saffy and her sister, dressed up

42

in cute Santa suits. I quickly like it. Saffy hates it if we miss a post.

Love it! I text back.

I turn my phone off. And vow that next year I'm going to escape from Saffy and find a way to make Hannah my friend. If she'll forgive me for being so useless. What would Anne Frank think of me? And then I feel guilty for even imaging that Anne Frank would care about my pathetic friendship problems.

The kitchen is invaded by guests. Mum makes sure everyone has a drink, and holds her glass up high.

"Happy Christmas, everyone," she says. "Let's drink to friendship, togetherness and joy! Cheers!"

"Cheers!"

Everyone is happy and enjoying themselves. So I paint on a false, fake smile and join in.

CHAPTER SEVEN

EVIE

Amina has finally spoken to Mo Ahmed from 9P, the boy she's been crushing on all year. Miraculously he was at a family wedding over the holiday. And not-so-miraculously he turned out to be a sexist pig.

"Just imagine!" she's telling me. "I look across the room, and it's him! Like, I could literally smell the aftershave! So I spent the whole evening sending him subtle messages with my eyelash extensions…"

"Which are completely lush– "

"And eventually he came over and told me off

for being immodest, and not a good Muslim girl. So naturally, I told him to buzz off."

We laugh a lot about it, and I think about telling her about my elf-encounter with Luke Braybourne before Christmas and how he asked for my snapchat, but somehow I don't. We gossip about Mum's new job instead and all the random celebs she might meet. Amina is dead impressed.

So I feel quite good, walking home. I've nailed the first day of term and I'm feeling kind of proud of Mum actually, when I walk past the Tube station and see it.

Her, not it. A massive billboard with a giant photo of my mum, wearing silky pink pyjamas, full face of make-up, bright pink mouth and spidery lashes, wrapping her mouth round a bagel.

I pinch my arm, but I am not hallucinating. I wish I was. Giant Mum is towering over me, over everyone coming out of the Tube station. It's a poster for her new show and the slogan reads:

BREAKFAST WITH BEX.
WAKE UP WITH A FRIEND
COMING SOON TO METRO RADIO. 7 TILL 10

"Oh my God!" It's Lottie, straight off the train. She must have finished school early. Perfect timing, I actually need a sister with me to take in this gigantic horror.

"I know, right?" I say. "*Wake up with a friend*? Like Mum's going to sleep with the whole country?"

Lottie groans. "No one's going to think … I mean … it's *Mum*."

I force myself to take a picture of the billboard because I can't quite believe it. OK, I think; how to spin this? I need to make it funny, fast. I have to own this, before everyone else sees it and I'm the butt of everyone's jokes.

I Instagram the picture with the caption: *When your Mum wins the Embarrassing Parent of the Year award and it's January 4 #cringe #ohnomumplease #wakeupwithafriend? #what?*

"I suppose we ought to be proud of her," says

Lottie, chewing her lip and staring at the poster.

"I am proud of her! It's an amazing job. I just wish she would be, you know, quieter about it." I shake my head.

"Wake up with a friend! People get paid to write slogans and that's what they come up with?"

"Could you do any better?"

"I totally could," I say, as we head for home. "And I can guarantee it would be about 1000% less embarrassing."

When we get home, Mum's in the living room, showing off a new outfit. She's had a haircut – *another* haircut – and is wearing make-up even though it's the middle of the day. She's taking selfies with her new iPhone, which was our Christmas present to her, in an attempt to drag her into the twenty-first century.

Mum is a total dinosaur when it comes to technology. Imagine a Tyrannosaurus Rex with a 1999 Nokia clasped in its little paws. That's Mum. She prides herself on it. "Twitter? Is that some sort of a bird-watching group?" she'll ask. "Facebook?

What is this book?"

Now here she is, selfie-ing away like your average ten-year-old.

Her audience is Dad, who's been driving for ten hours and is trying to stifle his yawns, and McGonagall, looking unimpressed on a cushion.

"Hello, girls!" she says. "I went shopping on the way home with Felicity, the stylist for Metro. What do you think?"

She's wearing a clingy dress in raspberry pink.

"It's lovely," says Lottie.

"It's lovely if you want to look like a giant sausage," I say, more accurately. "Which is good for the breakfast theme, I suppose."

Mum ignores me. "It's a bit fitted, but I like it. Felicity says I'm a spring."

"What do you mean, a spring? Like a babbling brook? Or a bouncing coil?" says Dad, who regrets it immediately when Mum starts explaining how Felicity the stylist decides which season you are, from your eye colour and skin tone – "You, Evie, would be winter, and Lottie's more summer" (natch).

"Mum, this is all great," Lottie breaks in patiently. "But we need to talk about the posters. Did you know the slogan was going to be *wake up with a friend*? Don't you think that might be a bit, you know, inappropriate?"

"I'm going to get some rest," says Dad. "With or without a friend."

Mum shrugs. "The team write the slogans," she says.

"I can think of better slogans than that," I say. "BREAKFAST WITH BEX: BLANDER THAN BANTER."

"Meanie!" Mum's mock-outraged, but I can see she wants to laugh.

"BREAKFAST WITH BEX: YOU'VE HIT THE SNOOZE BUTTON."

"Evie!" But she starts giggling.

"BREAKFAST WITH BEX: SHE"LL SCRAMBLE YOUR MIND, NOT YOUR EGGS."

I've done it, she's properly laughing.

"You are a horrible child," she says. "It's a good thing I love you." She holds out her new phone. "Look, here are the other posters."

We look. We groan. Same pyjamas. Same grin. The slogan is BREAKFAST WITH BEX: HAVE A HUG FROM YOUR RADIO.

"And then there's this one…"

Mum with coffee and a sausage on a fork. BREAKFAST WITH BEX: SOMETHING FOR EVERYONE.

"I thought you were cutting out processed meat!" says Lottie.

"I didn't eat it! I just held it. I *am* giving up processed meat!"

I check my Instagram. Lots of people laughing at my joke. Laughing with me, not at me – for now, at least. "They've set up all those accounts for me," says Mum. "Instabook and twitface and snapapp and what's off."

We try not to laugh. I make mental notes for my next routine.

"Can't they do it for you?" asks Lottie.

"I hate those boring celebrity accounts though, when it's obviously not the real person," I say. "Mum should totally run her own accounts."

"Well, that's what I thought," says Mum. "It'll

feel more genuine and authentic that way."

"Do you actually know how it works though?" asks Lottie. She sounds worried. "It's a lot of work."

So we talk her through it, right from how to log on (her password for Insta is Lottie!07 and for Twitter Evie?08, which is kind of cute). We explain how to block people who are weird and snooze people who are boring and hide posts and all of that stuff that comes naturally to us but seems to baffle old people.

Afterwards, I feel pretty good. We've helped Mum and hopefully stopped her being too embarrassing on Twitter. Job done.

I wish we'd thought a bit more. I wish we'd known a lot more.

I wish we'd realized how much there is to be scared of.

CHAPTER EIGHT

LOTTIE

"Hannah – Hannah – wait!"

It's amazing how difficult it is to actually speak to someone you're at school with, even though you share the same space for hours and hours every day. School is not made for private, difficult conversations. They treat us like a herd of sheep, forever together, shepherded from classroom to classroom.

But today, Hannah is right ahead of me. Only she's heading in the opposite direction from the girls streaming into the main hall for assembly.

She turns round. "What do you want? I'm late!"

"You're late?"

"Jewish assembly." She looks at me coldly and doesn't stop walking. I trot after her down the corridor. "We get together and talk about how rich we are."

"Hannah, look, I'm so sorry – I wanted to say something that day. I was just scared."

"That's just…" She searches for a word. "Completely inadequate. Your friends are racists. You said and did nothing. And why are you apologizing now? It was weeks ago."

"I wanted to." My voice sounds weak. "My mum – she's Jewish, but we never really identified with it, and…"

"Oh, spare me," says Hannah. She's reached her destination, the geography room. A post-it on the door says "Jewish Assembly". She pushes the door open and disappears inside.

I hesitate for half a second, and then follow her.

There are about forty girls in the room, and they are all looking at me. Two teachers at the front, Ms Stein, my maths teacher and another one who I think teaches history.

"Are you here for the assembly?" asks Ms Stein.

"Yes," I say, making up my mind. "Yes, I am."

There's a chair next to Hannah. I sit down, ignoring the way she's glaring at me. A girl reads something out, about the Bible story when Moses warns the Egyptians about the ten plagues – "like a horror film", she says. This is familiar – I loved the film *The Prince of Egypt* when I was younger. She's talking about the Pharaoh and his response to the plagues. It's all about leadership, and free will, and how if you make too many bad decisions you lose your ability to make good ones.

It's interesting, but I can't concentrate. I wonder how many bad decisions I've made. Am I weak and evil, like the Pharoah? After the speech they sing a song in Hebrew – everyone seems to know it. Then someone says a string of Hebrew words, and then people hand out food. Biscuits and crisps and little chocolate Danish pastries. Hannah turns her back on me and talks to her friends.

I take a biscuit from a smiley sixth former. I don't want it, but there doesn't seem to be an option to say no.

"I don't think we've seen you before," she says. "I'm Chloe. Who are you?"

Hannah laughs nastily. "Don't talk to her, Chloe! She's a complete antisemite, and she's only here to make fun of us with her racist friends."

The buzz of conversation stops, like the silence after you swat a wasp.

Everyone looks at me. My hands are shaking, my palms are sweaty, and I accidentally crush the biscuit into a fistful of crumbs.

I could turn and run, I think. But then I think of weak, cruel Pharaoh, and Moses finding the strength to speak up against him. Not that I'm quite sure who is Moses and who is Pharaoh in this situation.

"I am Jewish," I say. "At least, my mum is. My friends were really horrible to Hannah, and I was ashamed ... and I didn't find the right words then. But I really want to say sorry." I take a deep breath. "And also that I want to come to assembly and learn more about being Jewish."

I'm not sure where that last bit comes from. But I know as I say it that it's true.

They all watch me and I cringe. But then Chloe says, "I think that was very brave," and Ms Stein says, "You're very welcome here, Lottie," and Hannah kind of shrugs. And then everyone starts talking to their friends again.

"I really am so sorry," I say to Hannah. "You were brilliant when I had my asthma attack, and I never even thanked you properly."

"Why do you hang out with those girls? That's what I don't understand," she says.

"I didn't know anyone when I started school. I don't know if you remember, but I got a chest infection, right at the start of Year Seven, and had to stay off school for two weeks." When I came back everyone was in tight little groups, and I had two terms of feeling wheezy, tired, awkward and alone. Then I joined the tennis club.

"Saffy was the first person who was nice to me, and suddenly I was in her group and then – well and then I just got scared to leave. What if no one else wanted to be friends with me?" I spoke all in a rush, then looked down at my lap. When I said it out loud, it sounded so unconvincing.

"I get it," says Hannah. "I knew loads of people when I came here. I can imagine it was hard if you didn't."

It's OK, I can tell. Hannah's anger has drained away. She holds out the biscuit plate to me. "Have a rugelach," she says, and then when I look blank, she says, "The chocolate pastries."

I take one.

"I'm sorry, I was an idiot," she says. "It's asking a lot, to stand up to your friends."

"You weren't an idiot at all," I say. "I *should* have said something."

She looks at me for a moment and then she says, "Do you want to come round to my house after school?"

I hesitate, and she says, "Please do," so I say, "OK," and she grins in such a friendly way that it's hard to remember how angry she was.

CHAPTER NINE

EVIE

Amina and I stay after school in the Learning Resource Centre. She's got a history project to finish, and I'm trying to write new material. It's a routine about being the Doughnut Queen, and Mum being the new Voice of Nice, and it's kind of fun, in fact I start laughing at my own jokes, and then Amina wants to see them and she laughs too, and all the older kids revising for exams start telling us to shut up, and Ms Robbins the LRC manager says we are a Disruptive Force and on a warning.

I love the idea of being a Disruptive Force. But

Amina actually cares about stuff like behaviour points, so we leave.

"Come back to mine and hang out?" I say.

"I need to do my homework. Loads of maths and history."

"You're so try-hard. Whatever happened to the old Amina, who didn't care about grades and marks and all that?"

Amina looks a bit embarrassed. "Thing is, we're in Year Nine now."

"So?"

"*So*, I need to get good results. It's all very well for you, Evie. But people like me – brown people, Muslim people – we have to work a bit harder, do a bit better, to get good jobs. It's just a fact of life."

I sigh. "Well, I don't care about exams and stuff because I am not going to go down that conventional route. I'm going to be a comedy star."

She's smiling, but there's something a bit odd about her smile.

"Who's that?" she says, changing the subject

60

and pointing at a lanky boy walking across the playground towards us.

It's Luke! I gulp.

"Luke Braybourne," I say, trying to sound super casual. "Year Ten. You remember, from that debate thing we went to. Like, the tallest person in school. He must get bored of pigeons dive-bombing his nose."

She laughs and slightly raises her left eyebrow. "Oh, him," she says.

Luke reaches us.

"Hi, Evie," he says," how's it going? Hi, err…"

"It's going really well," I say, enthusiastically.

"I'm Amina," says my friend, with a dazzling smile. "We came to your debate club a few times. I loved your speech about welfare cuts."

I side-eye her. A minute ago she couldn't remember who he was. Now suddenly she's the debate club expert.

My phone pings. A text from Mum, demanding that I come home right away.

"Better go," I say. "The diva has spoken."

"Diva?" says Luke, looking confused.

"Evie's mum is Bex Harris, the Voice of Nice on Metro Radio," says Amina.

"That's cool," he says.

The phone pings again. "I guess I'd better go," I say, hoping that Luke will offer to walk with me.

"Me too," says Amina, "I've got a ton of homework."

Luke walks with us to the school gate. Amina and I turn right, towards our homes, he turns left towards the high street.

But after a minute, Amina stops. "I forgot, Mum wants me to go to the shops first," she says. And before I can offer to go with her, she's hurrying away in the opposite direction.

When I walk through the door, there are two suitcases in the hallway and I nearly fall over them.

Voices coming from the kitchen. I push open the door. Mum's there, and another woman, and a boy who looks a bit older than me. They're drinking tea and chatting – that is, Mum and the woman are chatting, the boy is reading a book and listening to music judging by the air pods stuck in his ears.

"Evie, darling!" says Mum. "Sarah, this is Evie, my youngest by two minutes!"

"Hello, Evie!" Sarah is Mum's age, I guess. She has grey hair, in a sharp bob which is longer at the front, and a heavy fringe. She has perfectly groomed eyebrows, and dark red lipstick, green top and tailored trousers. She looks exactly like my imaginary future agent. Sharp, elegant, in control.

"This is Noah," Sarah says, gesturing at the boy, who nods briefly at me. Huh. Rude. I don't bother saying hello to him, he obviously can't hear me.

Noah has wild curly hair, a crumpled T-shirt and holey jeans. He's got a wide mouth that looks like it's made for laughing, but right now is clamped shut in a scowl.

"Sarah and Noah are literally just off the Eurostar from Paris," says Mum. "I was at St Pancras for a meeting with Fiona, and we just bumped into each other, and I insisted they came here for a cup of tea and a chat before going to their hotel. Isn't it lovely! I haven't seen Sarah for, gosh, thirty years, isn't it?"

"We were at school together," Sarah explains. "And not just school, FZY and Maccabi, and BBYO, and UJS…"

"What are those things?"

Sarah raises one elegant eyebrow. "Jewish youth groups. You don't send your girls to them, Bex?"

I'm about to explain that we don't really go in for Jewish stuff, when Mum rushes in. "Oh well, south London, you know, not much going on."

"I sent Noah to summer camp every year, all the way from Paris," says Sarah. "And now we are moving to London, I'd like him to go to school with some of the friends he's made, but it's impossible to find a place. All the Jewish schools in north London are full up, and we can't afford private until I find a job here."

"I'm so pleased you're moving back! You've been in Paris for so long!"

"That's what happens when you fall in love with a Frenchman. We've been there since Noah was little."

"But now…?"

"It's complicated," says Sarah. "I hope my husband will join us in London, but you know, with Brexit and everything…"

Mum clearly wants to dive in and ask lots of nosy questions, but controls herself.

"It's a pity you can't call on Old Girl privilege and get our school to squeeze him in, but it's still all girls."

"What's it like there now, Evie?" asks Sarah. "The uniform's changed a bit."

"No, no, it's Lottie that's at our school," says Mum, while I seethe silently. "Wait till she's home, Sarah, the uniform's exactly the same. Those awful white blouses – they look a lot better on her than they ever did on me. Although, hang on, it's Wednesday. She's got tennis after school."

"Remember Miss Wilkes and that time when the balls went missing?" And they rock with laughter, while I make myself some toast and peanut butter.

"So where do you go to school, Evie?" asks Sarah once she remembers that I'm in the room.

"Just the school up the road," I say.

"A really good local state school," says Mum firmly.

"No bullying?" asks Sarah. "Because in Paris, I wouldn't touch the state options."

It's sad that Mum's elegant friend appears to be a total snob. I get myself a full fat Coke from the fridge and take a swig.

"Nope," says Mum. "What's the rush for Noah to start school over here?"

Sarah just shakes her head. "He needs to leave. It's just not comfortable for us any more. Even his dad agrees."

Noah's head jerks up, and I realize he's been listening all along.

"Dad needs to leave too," he says. "It's not safe for him to stay."

"What happened?" I can't help it, I'm way too much like Mum at times.

"There was an ... an incident," says Sarah. Noah rolls his eyes and picks up his book. It's by someone called Primo Levi and it's called *If This is a Man*. I've never heard of it.

"How difficult," says Mum. "And now you've

got a week to look at flats, and job hunt, *and* find a school?"

"I've been thinking about it for a long time. Putting feelers out. I'm sure I can find something. There must be a school. And my mother is still in Edgware, I can stay with her. But she's in a flat now, and there's no room for Noah – it's difficult."

I know what Mum's going to say before she even says it.

"Well, of course, Noah can stay with us! Just until you get yourself sorted out. And I bet he could go to Evie's school for a while, we can speak to the head tomorrow. It's better than nothing!"

Gee, thanks Mum.

"Really?" says Sarah. "Are you sure? Because that would be very helpful."

I mumble something about homework and go on up to my room.

And then it hits me. A strange French boy, who seems rude and unfriendly, living in our house, going to my school?

Non, merci, s'il vous plaît…

CHAPTER

NINE

CHAPTER TEN

LOTTIE

All through geography, all through maths, I'm thinking about what I'm going to say to Saffy. My heart beats fast, my stomach churns. But I can't avoid it. It has to be done.

We finish maths, and we're packing up our things. Saffy's got the locker next to me, and she's going on and on about tennis. I feel bad, because I like tennis, and I like being on the team – I worked hard for that – but I'll have to sacrifice it. I heave my bag on to my shoulder, leaving my PE kit in the locker.

She whistles at me. "You need your stuff. And

your tennis shoes. Don't tell me you forgot about practice." She rolls her eyes. "Good thing you've got me to remind you."

"I'm not coming," I say, voice only shaking slightly.

She stares. "What do you mean *you're not coming*?"

"I've got something else to do."

"Is it something to do with your mum?" asks Topaz, who has the next locker along.

Saffy, Topaz and Mel think it's amazing that my mum is now – according to them – a celebrity. They don't know whether to suck up to me about it ("Do you think we'll be invited to parties at Metro? Or the Metro Festival – can you get free tickets?") or tease me. ("When your mum's on *Strictly Come Dancing*, I hope she can dance better than you do, Lottie!")

"No, it's not," I say.

"Well, what is it then?" Saffy's impatient. "Get a move on!"

"I should have said this a long time ago, but I don't like the way you talk about people." My voice is very soft, but I keep going. "I don't like the way you talk about Jewish people, or Muslim people or anyone different from you." (I'd say Black people too, but there aren't really any at our school for Saffy to be mean about, which probably tells you a lot about our school.)

"*What?*" Saffy's mouth is a perfect circle.

"I haven't ever liked it, but I've been too much of a coward to say so. But actually, when you insult Jewish people, you're insulting me too. Because I am Jewish. Mum is Jewish, and that means I am too. And when you insult us, and Muslim people and Hindu people, and Asian people in general, you just show yourself up as … as … a bigot. And I don't want to be friends with a bigot."

"You can't say that!" Saffy's face is bright pink, and her eyes are sparkling with tears. "That's libel! I could actually sue you for that. You need to take it back, Lottie. Or I'm going to make your life hell."

It feels like we're alone in the corridor, it's so quiet. I'm actually shaking. But then Hannah, three lockers along, says, "Well done, Lottie," and Aslesha Kumar, who is in 8D and so cool I've never dared speak to her, says, "It wouldn't be libel, it'd be slander, and it isn't either because it's all true. My mum's a lawyer."

And then lots of people start clapping, and Saffy grabs her tennis racket and says, "I hate you, Lottie Harris," and runs away down the corridor. Topaz dithers for a moment and then runs after her.

"Are you all right?" asks Hannah.

"Yeah."

Actually, I feel great. I've spoken up for myself. Not just for myself, but for other people as well. And right now, I don't care what the consequences are.

CHAPTER ELEVEN

LOTTIE

From the outside, Hannah's house is a bit like ours, squashed in the middle of a terrace, with a black-and-white chequered path and a blue front door. Inside, I smell cinnamon and fresh bread. The walls are covered in pictures. Some are paintings, some are framed posters, some are photographs. In the hallway there are so many that you can hardly see that the walls are painted beetroot pink.

I spot one of Hannah as a little girl in dungarees, and another of her lined up with a younger sister and two older brothers. I guess this was at her batmitzvah, because she's definitely wearing some make-up, and a dress – red and sticky-out – under a black jacket.

I didn't think you wore skirts, I think, but I don't say. I don't feel I know Hannah well enough to pry.

The kitchen is full of noise and people – a younger sister, Dalya, an older brother, Sam. Hannah's mum, on the phone with one hand, taking a cake out of the oven with the other, music playing on speakers. Everyone's nice and friendly and we take cans from the fridge and go up to Hannah's room, which has lime green walls and a pinboard covered with photos.

We flop on to beanbags on the floor and then we talk. I tell Hannah about how Mum isn't keen to even talk about growing up Jewish.

"Do you know why?" Hannah asks.

"She just…" I think about it. "She says she wants to leave the past behind. But my dad wants us to know about our heritage. So he takes us to places like the tower in York, where…" I break off. It's horrible to even think about.

"Clifford's Tower," says Hannah, "We went there." We're both quiet, thinking about what happened in York hundreds of years ago, back in medieval times. All the Jewish people in the town huddled inside the building, listening to an angry mob outside threatening to kill them. The Jews who killed themselves rather than be murdered.

"Mum wouldn't come with us," I remember. "She stayed in a café, said she had some calls to make." Thinking about it now I remember how anxious Mum was when we came back, to move the conversation on to whether we wanted pizza or pasta that night, and the film we were going to see later.

"It's so different to the way I've grown up," says Hannah. "We're just *so* Jewish."

"Tell me what being *so* Jewish is like."

She ticks things off on her fingers. "One, going to shul. Two, keeping kosher. Three, living in the bubble. All my friends are Jewish apart from at school, although obviously Lucy and Nina, Annie and Scarlett in our year, I've known since we were in the womb…"

"Oh. Wow. Um," I say.

"Four, youth group. Five, tzedakah – that means charity – I volunteer at my shul's drop in centre for asylum seekers. Six, we go to Israel every year. Seven, since my batmitzvah I've carried on studying, and I can pretty much daven – that means *pray* – the whole musaf – that means *additional* – service, not that anyone lets me at my shul. Girls, you know. Post batmitzvah, there's nothing for us."

"Nothing?" I'm disappointed. And also, my head is spinning from all the unfamiliar words.

Hannah laughs. "My mum would tell me off for saying that! There are lots of opportunities to study. She's training to be a rabbi. So, what's your list?"

"Can women be rabbis?" I kind of thought you had to be a man and have a long beard.

"Yes, in progressive movements – the more modern ones, like Reform. And there isn't this mad difference between men and women at all." Hannah's voice sounds sad. "And in Orthodox synagogues like ours, you can, but it's very

76

unusual." She takes a swig of her drink. "Do your family do anything Jewish at all?"

I take a deep breath. "One, sometimes we light Chanucah candles. Two, Mum makes honey cake around the time of the Jewish new year. Three, Mum buys bagels sometimes and we have them with smoked salmon and cream cheese. Four, at Passover – is that what it's called? – she buys matzah crackers."

"Ah," says Hannah. "Judaism through the medium of food. Maybe it's the best way."

We get on with our homework after that, and then I need to go, so I'm back for supper, but on the Tube home I feel so good, to have a way to talk about Jewish stuff without it being all about death and murder and horror. I'm pleased that I have a friend like Hannah.

But when I get off the Tube and switch on my phone, there are angry messages from Saffy and Topaz and Mel. And they say things like "You bully" and "We're reporting you" and "Get lost, loser" and worse. And I don't feel so brave any more.

CHAPTER TWELVE

LOTTIE

Over supper, Mum breaks the news that some French boy called Noah might be coming to stay.

"What could I say?" she asks, but it's one of those questions we're not meant to answer. "The poor boy, he's had such a difficult time. And it's only temporary. Sarah's very resourceful. She'll have a job in no time, and find him a place in a school in north London."

"You might have asked us first," says Dad.

"I'm sorry! Sorry! But I knew you'd all be lovely about it." She tangles spaghetti around her fork. "He keeps kosher, though, so we'll have to eat more vegetarian."

She sees Evie's appalled face. "I mean it's good to cut out meat, isn't it? It's so bad for you. And for the poor animals."

"No meat!" says Evie, as though Mum's suggesting we give up oxygen. "That's inhumane!"

"What are you talking about, it's more humane!"

"It's inhumane to us! I love meat! I didn't know kosher meant vegetarian, anyway."

"It doesn't," says Mum, "but there are all kinds of rules about what meat you can have, and it comes from a special butcher, and you need special plates and cutlery, and you can't eat it with milk products, and it's too difficult. So we'll stick to veggie mince and curry and things like that."

"It sounds like a religion invented by someone with an eating disorder," says Evie, with that look on her face that she gets when she's about to start writing a comedy routine. "Like the Jewish God of OCD…"

"Don't joke about mental health," says Mum, glancing at me in that scared way she has sometimes, as though I'm a fragile vase, liable to topple off a mantelpiece.

"I'd like to know more about the rules," I say, partly because I do, and partly because I'm curious to know how Mum will react.

She shakes her head and says, "Believe me, you really don't. He'll go and stay with Sarah and his grandmother for weekends," she says, "so it's just weekdays, while he's at school. We'll hardly notice he's here."

"You might not," says Evie, "but I certainly will. If he's going to be at my school."

"He won't be in your year," Mum says. "He's fifteen. He'll be in Year Ten."

"He's missed a whole term," says Dad. "Difficult to catch up, I'd have thought."

"Super-bright," says Mum. "That's partly why Sarah wants to bring him here. And partly because things have been difficult there in Paris."

"To put it mildly," says Dad, and Mum shoots him a look that means, *not now*.

"If this boy is going to live here," Evie says, "and go to my school, surely we've got the right to know why. Are his parents splitting up?"

"No…" says Mum. "Not exactly." Again, that quick glance towards me. Again, the toppling vase.

"We should tell them," says Dad. "After all, Noah probably will."

Mum doesn't say anything. She just shrugs. "Noah and his father got beaten up," says Dad. "On their way to synagogue. It wasn't pleasant, and it affected Noah badly. Maybe he'll talk about it one day, but you let him get there in his own time, OK?"

Evie's eyes are amazed. "Sure, OK."

Mum's eyes are on me. "OK, Lottie?"

"Of course, I won't say anything."

I thought I was being brave, standing up to Saffy. But now I realize. I didn't even know what being brave was.

After we've all finished, Evie and I are left to clear up, while Mum and Dad get the spare room ready. Noah's coming to stay tomorrow. There were a few months when Mum and Dad thought they'd have to have a lodger in that room, when Dad lost his job, but then he started driving. I never really talked to Dad about how he feels about driving the Uber, although I know he must miss his job in theatre. Maybe it's because I feel bad that so much of what he earns goes on my school fees.

"Noah's kind of gorgeous," says Evie. "Mad curly hair. Big dark eyes."

"Hmm," I say. I don't really think about boys like that. Maybe I will one day. Right now, I suspect I'm asexual. I can't even imagine what it's like to fancy someone.

"But he's also rude. Like, he didn't say one word to me. He just read his book."

I think about what it must feel like to come to another country because you've been beaten up. Leaving your dad behind, where he might get attacked again. Leaving all your friends and everything you know. And having to go to Evie's school and stay with strangers.

"Maybe it's all a bit much."

Evie stacks the last plate in the dishwasher. "Yeah, maybe. And what a pain about him being all religious and kosher."

"It's not such a problem," I say. "Maybe it's something we could try."

Evie rolls her eyes. "You're not getting religious on me, are you? You're annoying enough already."

"I'm just interested."

She scowls at me. "Why do you always have to be *better* than everyone else?"

I don't bother answering. The washing up is done. Evie can take the rubbish out for once. I go up to my room.

I start on my history homework. It's all about the Holocaust this term. I have to do a presentation about Auschwitz. I've written most of it, but I need to insert pictures.

So I look at piles of corpses. I look at people jammed into bunk beds. I look at skeletal bodies, at gas chambers where millions of people were killed like vermin, I look at faces of people who could have been Mum and Evie and me.

I feel my lungs tighten. A wheeze escapes my

lips. *Stop it*, I tell myself. *Stop making it about you. Stop it.*

I shut off my laptop and phone, and take my inhaler and lie on my bed, doing the breathing exercises that ought to help. In – two, three, four. Out – two, three, four. I'm struggling for control, but after a while I achieve it. My lungs relax. The wheezing stops. I'm OK.

I lie on the bed and stare at the ceiling and I wish that I was Evie and I didn't have lungs that squeezed the air out of me.

But then Evie could have been the twin that got asthma and that would be awful for her.

I want to do something worthwhile. So that even if I do die young, I'll have changed the world.

I think about climate change. I think about Anne Frank, writing her diary. And I think about how she died, and where she died, in a concentration camp, and how she was just one of millions of Jews that died.

And I think, there's a gap in the world that those Jewish people should fill. I am Jewish, according to Dad, one-hundred per cent Jewish if I choose to be, and that's one person more against all those that were killed.

So, maybe that's a choice I can make. Maybe I should try being Jewish. Maybe that would count for something.

Maybe then I'd feel less scared of living.

CHAPTER THIRTEEN

EVIE

I've never met anyone so dedicated to his air pods as Noah. Honestly, he has them in his ears all day every day. Apart from in the shower – I assume – which is where he is now, right when I need to be. (Not with him, obviously. Completely by myself.)

I bang on the door and he sidles out a full five minutes later, with a towel wrapped around his middle, showing off a light brown chest with quite impressive muscle tone. The pods are jammed into his ears. Maybe they are waterproof.

He keeps them in all through breakfast (munching toast and reading his book), and when we're walking to school together. He hardly looks at me. The pods sit in his ears like giant insects, burrowing into his brain.

He arrived last night after supper, clearly not very happy about it, and disappeared into his room as soon as he could. I'm meant to be taking him to the school office.

And now we're walking together through the drizzle, not talking. We pass several of my friends, who all clock the nice-looking boy at my side, and then realize he's not actually talking to me. It's like walking some posh dog who completely outclasses you.

I see Luke Braybourne walking towards us. "Evie!" he says, smiling. (That smile! So adorable!) He looks at Noah and waits politely for an introduction.

I nudge Noah in the side. "This is Noah," I say. "From France. Staying with us. Air pods permanently inserted."

Noah sighs and takes them out. "This is

Luke," I say, "a friend from school. He's in your year, so you might even be in some of the same classes."

"Hello, Luke," says Noah. His accent is really nice to listen to, I have to admit.

"Nice to meet you," says Luke, and we walk together towards the school gates. I wish Noah wasn't here. Then I could impress Luke with my scintillating conversation and persuade him to date me, a girl from Year Nine who's about a mile shorter than he is, and is known to all as the Doughnut Queen.

I say, "So, what have you been up to?" at exactly the same time as Luke says, "It's debating club on Friday, would you like…"

"I'd love to," I say.

"Do you want to come along too?" he says to Noah. "We debate current affairs and politics."

"Maybe," says Noah, shrugging. "Aren't we meant to be going to the office, Evie?"

"We are," I say, just as the school bell goes. It's like being caught in a stampede of wild buffalo. Luke gets swept away in the rush. "See you Friday … and bring Amina…" I hear, over the noise of the crowd.

"Come on, then," I say to Noah. But he doesn't answer. He's plugged in again.

CHAPTER FOURTEEN

LOTTIE

I'm worried about seeing Saffy and Topaz and Mel in the mornings, but Hannah and I work out a strategy. I meet her outside school, and we walk in together. She goes slightly ahead of me to check out the locker area. Then she rushes back to let me know that it's clear, and I can safely get my stuff for the day.

And luckily, Saffy and the others aren't there at all. I forget all about them as we file down to assembly, as Hannah's telling me about something funny that her brother did last night. It's only when we're sitting down, and I turn around and see Saffy's cold, blue eyes staring straight through me, that I remember how angry she is. And how scary.

But I soon forget all about her. The head of year announces that as it's Holocaust Memorial Day, there are two speakers visiting the school today. Beside Mrs Elliot, the head teacher, they look tiny, but then she is a giant – when *Game of Thrones* was on, people used to call her Brienne of Tarth. They must both be less than five foot, an old man and woman, smiling down at us.

"Girls, we're very privileged today to have two special guests," says Mrs Elliot in her most syrupy voice, the voice she usually uses to tell us about Old Girls who have got into Oxford or Cambridge, or become British Ambassador to Uzbekistan or discovered a cure for an obscure disease. "They are here on Holocaust Memorial Day to tell you about their experiences as child refugees. They came to Britain on something called the Kindertransport – special trains which brought Jewish children to safety in Britain on the eve of World War Two. Please listen very carefully to their story."

The man speaks first. His name is Albert Wright, he says, but he was born Albrecht Reich in Germany, to a family who "were more German than Jewish". He shows us a medal, a dark metal cross. "This is the Iron Cross that my father won fighting for Germany in the First World War. It did him no good when they came to take him away."

Albert tells us about Kristallnacht in 1938, when Jewish shops and businesses were attacked, their windows broken, their contents looted. The great synagogue in Hanover, his home town, was burned to the ground. That night he lay awake, hearing his parents talking, trying to block out their words. "No one wants to think their parents are scared," he said.

That was when his parents decided to send him on the Kindertransport to England, wrapping the Iron Cross carefully and putting it into his suitcase. They said goodbye with hugs at the station and he boarded the train. He never saw them again.

I try to imagine saying goodbye to Mum and Dad, getting on to a train and leaving them behind. I can almost see the shards of glass lying on the streets, smell the ashes dancing in the air.

Albert arrived in London. Every child had to be sponsored – "It cost them fifty pounds, which is the equivalent of about three thousand pounds now" – and his sponsor was Mr Smith who lived in a big house in Hampstead. Albert never met Mr Smith; he was looked after by his housekeeper, and then packed off to Kent, to a hostel for refugee boys. He was thirteen and quite alone in the world.

His wife, Anna, takes over with her story. She was younger when she came to England, just ten. Her parents put her on the train in Hamburg with cuddles and kisses, and told her to look out of the window at the next station. When she did, they were there on the platform, waving and blowing kisses. "They must have raced there in their car," she tells us. "And that was the last time I ever saw them."

Unlike Albert and most children who came on the Kindertransport, Anna knew the names and details of her sponsors – a friend of her parents had met them in London and asked them to take Anna. They were sisters. "I called them the Aunties," she says. "They treated me like I was their own." At first they got post from their parents, but then the letters stopped coming. After the war they found out that their parents had been deported and murdered. Anna talks about a letter she received from her father, one of the last he sent. "Live your life to the full," he wrote. "Be happy. Tell the truth. And do not grieve."

I'm jolted back into the present day by someone kicking the back of my chair. It's Saffy, of course. She leans forward.

"None of this is true," she whispers. "It's all made up. You know that, don't you?"

I don't know what to do, but I do know I can't listen to one more word without making a noise. So I stand up, and as quietly as I can leave the hall. I think no one's noticed, but Ms Stein comes after me, following me into the East corridor.

"Are you OK, Lottie?"

"I just felt … a bit breathless…"

"Asthma attack?" Do I dare tell her? Slowly, I shake my head.

"Did the talk upset you?"

I nod.

"It is upsetting, I know," she says, sympathetically, "but it's important to listen. My own parents were refugees."

It's never struck me before, but maybe someone in my family was a refugee too. I have no idea. Mum has never told me. I never asked.

"Miss," I say. "Saffy said – she told me – that none of it was true."

Miss Klein's eyebrows are fine and dark and arched, and they hit her fringe when I say this.

"Saffy Andrews?" she says. I nod.

"Come with me," she says. "Don't worry – you're not in any trouble. But if that's what Saffy said, it's very serious and we need to hear exactly what happened and deal with it."

I nod. I feel relieved. I've been brave again.

Maybe the more you practise, the easier it is. Or maybe it's about finding the right person to talk to, at the right time. Whatever, I feel pretty confident that Saffy won't be bothering me again.

CHAPTER FIFTEEN

EVIE

Ms Turnberry decided that our comedy competition showed a) "a lot of potential" and b) "a need to work more on material before it reaches the wider school community". So she's set up an after-school impro workshop, and allowed me to join. It's a great chance to try out my new material, even if it's just to an audience of six wannabe comedians, and a few of their friends. Including Amina, obviously and – oh my days! – Luke Braybourne, sitting next to her.

I can't believe he's come to see me. That's amazing. And he and Amina seem to be getting on really well too. I'm glad she likes him. I'm going to tell her about my secret crush soon – I don't think she'll laugh at me.

And it's my turn and I'm on the stage and I'm just buzzing with energy and confidence and excitement.

"So, hello," I say, "my name's Evie. Last time I was on this stage, someone threw a doughnut at me. Which was rubbish, because I prefer croissants."

That gets a laugh. Yes!

"You won't have heard of me. But you might have woken up in bed with my mum."

Ms Turnberry is frowning. Everyone is giggling and "oohing".

"You all have such dirty minds. My mum is Breakfast Bex. The new face of radio. There are giant posters of her all over town. Her task is to cheer people up first thing in the morning. She's the aural equivalent of scrambled eggs – tasty but also nutritious. She plays all the top grime artists, like Take That and Elton John."

I'm getting laughs, and a warm, appreciative

vibe. Luke laughs every time. I can see his teeth when he does.

"So, it's kind of weird because she talks about us a lot on the radio. Dad's called the Other Half. Me and my sister, we're known as Twin One and Twin Two. I wouldn't mind, but she's the one who picked our names. You'd think she could get them right!

"It's odd that she calls us that, because when you have twins, the main advice that parents get is to make sure your twins develop as individuals. Emphasize their uniqueness! It's funny because I bet no one does that when non-twin babies are born. Do parents get told, 'Make sure your kid knows who they are, so they don't get confused with the kid next door?' Are they told, 'Dress them differently from other people so they're clear about who they are?' It's as though people expect twins to have blurry edges. Anyway, no one could be more different than my sister and me – we're the world's least identical twins." And I go off into my old material, slightly improved from Doughnut Night.

"So, this Christmas I asked for boots, chocolate and false eyelashes. My sister asked for goats. Yes, goats. So, we've got a whole herd of them, munching the grass in the garden, waiting for her to raise the cash to ship them out to—"

The buzzer on Ms Turnberry's phone goes off. My time is up.

Everyone claps and cheers. I love comedy club. They love me.

"OK, let's have some feedback please. Remember to be constructive. Balance negative with positive."

Lots of hands up.

"You're just so funny! It's your face as much as anything you say. No, I mean it in a good way!"

"It should be more about you, less about your mum."

Some girl from 8W sticks up her hand. "You were great, babes. Loved it. But I thought you were kind of sexist about your mum at the beginning. I know those ads are grim but that's not her fault. They were clearly created by a male fantasist…"

"My dad," I say, and get the biggest laugh of the entire session.

Amina and Luke are waiting for me after Ms Turnberry's pep talk. ("Some good stuff, group! Really seeing improvements! Billy, clean up your language, please. Kevin, look up the meaning of the word "plagiarism".)

"You were brilliant!" says Amina, and Luke nods and smiles.

Amina is looking so pretty with her huge brown eyes and her shiny hair. Luke's looking good too; he's had a haircut, so you can see his kind eyes better. My hair is a ball of frizz, like the wire wool that Dad uses to block a hole in our wall where mice try and come in. My fringe is all sweaty. But he came to see me, didn't he? By some miracle, Luke Braybourne seems to like me.

"Thanks for coming along," I say to Luke, suddenly shy. "I hope it wasn't too boring."

"You were great!" he says. "Did your sister really ask for goats for Christmas?"

We walk together through the playground. I explain about the goats. Then Amina and Luke are talking about something that was on the news last night, but I'm not listening. I'm too happy.

"Hey, Evie."

Noah. Sitting on a wall, right outside the school.

"I was waiting. Where were you?"

"Oh, sorry," I say. "I didn't realize. I was at comedy club." He looks at me blankly. "Maybe we can all go and get a milkshake or something."

I mean with everyone, especially Luke, but he says he has to go home and so does Amina. I bet they were put off by Noah's scowling face.

"Forget the milkshake," I tell Noah. "Let's go."

We set off. "How was your first day anyway?" I say.

He shrugs – so French! – "It was OK. I won't be there long anyway."

His gloomy mood surrounds me, like a sudden fog on a sunny day. Talk about a buzz kill. "What's the matter?" I ask. But those airpods are back in his ears, and he doesn't even see my lips move.

CHAPTER SIXTEEN

EVIE

"Everyone, shut up!" says Luke Braybourne. "I mean ... silence please! Welcome to Debate Club!"

There's about thirty of us in the lecture theatre. Most are older than us, and there's a teacher supposedly supervising (actually marking essays in a corner). Amina and I are sitting in the front row, where Luke can't miss us. To my surprise I see Noah at the end of our row, with some other boys from his year.

"Today's debate," says Luke, "is about immigration. The title is *We Need Stricter Border Controls*."

I sneak a look around the room. I estimate that eighty-five per cent of the people here are from an immigrant background. There's Jemal, from my English set, across the room. He made everyone cry last term when he wrote a poem about leaving his family behind in Eritrea. Amina's grandparents came here from Pakistan. There's Wiktoria from Poland and Piotr from Lithuania.

My dad's family have lived in Hampshire for generations. But Mum's parents came from Europe … somewhere, some time. I'm a bit vague about the details. It's not something she talks about. I've never thought of myself as anything but British.

The debate begins. A girl called Sophie from Year Eleven is for the motion. "I'm not saying we shouldn't have immigration," he says. "Just that it needs to be controlled. We have a housing crisis in this country. An NHS crisis…"

"We need a wall!" yells out another boy, from the back row. "They have a wall in Hungary! They have a wall in the USA! Britain for the British!"

"Oi," says the teacher, looking up from his marking. "Calm it down. You're not in the Houses of Parliament."

Sophie carries on, talking about points systems, and people with criminal records who don't get deported, about how we should be able to decide who gets to live in our country. And then Luke makes the opposing speech, which is all about the huge amount of tax that immigrants pay, and the jobs they do, and the way they enrich our culture and how London and other cities have always been multicultural, and are better for it, and everyone cheers and then there's a vote, which is forty-five to three for Luke.

"That was excellent," says Amina. "People need to stand up for us." She sings the bit from *Hamilton* about immigrants getting the job done.

"My mum's family were immigrants too," I say, surprising myself.

"What, Viking immigrants?"

I must have mentioned the Viking DNA. "No, from Europe," I say.

"Oh. Where from?"

"I'm not even sure," I admit. I feel awkward, like I'm trying to share some sort of immigration connection when it was clearly so trauma-free that no one ever mentioned it. And then to change the subject, "What did you think of Luke?"

"He was very good," she says.

"I know…" I hesitate. I should tell her how I feel about him now – but just then he walks over.

"Hi, Evie, just wanted to thank you for coming," he says, "And you too, Amina." How polite is that? He's like a knight in shining armour, or someone off *Downton Abbey*.

"We enjoyed it," says Amina. "Great speech,"

He scratches his head, adorably unable to cope with a compliment. "Better go, I need to pick up a sandwich before next period."

"So do I," says Amina, "See you later, Evie." Before I know it they're walking away across the courtyard, heading for the mobile lunch kiosk.

"See you," I say, but they're out of earshot. I'm

so stupid. Why didn't I say I needed a sandwich too? OK, Amina knew I'd eaten one before the meeting but … hang on … so did she!

Oh, well. Amina can gather information for me. Even if she doesn't realize she's doing it.

Friendships aren't just about the things you share. They're also about the things that you don't – or can't talk about.

CHAPTER SEVENTEEN

LOTTIE

One of the annoying things about going to school miles away from home is that I have to get up earlier than anyone else. Well, not earlier than Mum, whose show on Metro starts at six a.m., but way earlier than Evie or Dad. And I'd assumed way earlier than Noah too, until I get up one morning at six and he's in the kitchen before me, sitting at the breakfast bar, laptop open, air pods in.

"Oh, sorry," I say automatically, before wondering what exactly I am apologizing for. I peel a banana and wonder if I need to make conversation. I've hardly spoken to Noah since he arrived.

"Are you getting on OK at school?" I ask. He takes out one pod.

"Yeah, I guess. Why don't you go to school with your sister?"

"I go to Mum's old school. Where your mum went too."

"Ah, the old school." He rolls his eyes. "Tennis and hockey and basket – no – netball. If Mum could send me there she would."

"They take boys in the sixth form."

"Don't tell her that!" He gives me a faint smile. "I prefer to be with my friends."

"Back in Paris?"

"No, here in London. North London. Mum sent me back here every summer to go to Jewish summer camp. You don't go?"

"No. Mum wouldn't have sent us to something like that. She's not really into Jewish stuff."

"She's not?" He sounds surprised.

"No, just –" I remember what Hannah said. "Judaism though the medium of food."

He laughs. But then he says, "I think she cares more than you think. She's been talking a lot to my mother. And she's going to open up about it on her radio show this morning. That's why I'm listening." He glances at his watch. "It's about time now."

He clicks on his laptop. Mum's voice fills the room.

"...*Sarah, a very old friend of mine is here from Paris. And I know, guys, this show is all about good news and feeling uplifted and happy, but indulge me for a minute. Because, after this ad break, I want to talk to you about something I feel very strongly about.*"

I stare at Noah. "She's not meant to talk about politics, or anything like that."

"That's Mum for you. She is incredibly persuasive," says Noah. "She's working on my dad right now, to get him to leave France. And it is important … shhh…"

Mum is on again. "*So, my friend Sarah's been telling me what it's like to be Jewish in France. And it's brought up something that I don't think many people realize…*"

She explains how although Jews make up less

than one per cent of the French population, more than half of the racist crimes committed there are carried out against them. Things like swastikas painted on Jewish graves, people attacked as they leave synagogue, a young man who was tortured and killed. An old lady killed by her neighbours. On housing estates, in modern Paris. Not in Nazi times, just a few years ago.

Jews held hostage in a supermarket which sold Jewish food. Four of them were shot dead. Killed for being Jewish.

Then suddenly she says, *"Now I know it's not your usual breakfast fare, but this means a lot to me because of my family history. And we should all be alert, in this country as well. The past is not as far away as we think."* A tiny pause, then, *"I promise I'll be back with something more cheerful after this classic number from Elton John."* And "Your Song" fills the kitchen.

Noah turns the sound off. "Wow," he says. "She was amazing. You should be proud."

"I am. I think." I *am* proud. But I do wonder if Mum talking about murders comes under her brief of Voice of Nice, when people tune in for heartwarming stories about kittens and marathon-running grannies.

And then I realize that it's time for me to leave the house, so I say goodbye and head for the Tube.

I'm in maths when a right-wing politician says that Mum's type controls the media. I'm in geography when a left-wing MP says on Twitter that radio presenters who believe in killing Palestinian children shouldn't be given a voice on national radio.

But it isn't until I get home that I see the flood of poison that's gushed into the world through the pipes of social media. And it's not just directed at Mum.

Some of the comments, some of the threats, are directed at us as well.

CHAPTER EIGHTEEN

EVIE

I am *heartbroken*. I am *devastated*. I am *utterly betrayed*.

On Friday what did I see when I walked into the playground? Amina, hand in hand with Luke. I avoided her all day, but in the evening she called me, sounding all hushed and excited and shy. She and Luke went to a vegan café after school on Thursday. They talked about current affairs and politics and he told her how much he liked her. And now they are a couple. They're Lumina. Or Amuke.

"It just happened," she whispers on the

phone, "I had no idea Luke was even interested, we just got talking about politics and stuff, and then, I don't know, my hand brushed against his and there we were, hand in hand … and he's soooooooo amazing!"

And naturally all I can do is crack some more lame jokes about his height and say how pleased I am for her, when my heart is shattered into tiny pieces.

She didn't guess. I don't think so anyway. Why didn't I say that I liked him ages ago, before Christmas? Why didn't I put a massive TAKEN, HANDS OFF label on Luke?

Because I never thought he'd look at anyone in our year, that's why. Specifically me. I never even thought of Amina. But she's gorgeous and smart and funny, so *of course* he likes her. And naturally she likes him. Who wouldn't?

I watched Netflix for three hours last night and nothing made me laugh. Not even *Friends*. Mum and Dad and Lottie were talking for hours in the other room. They didn't even notice how miserable I was.

Today, Mum has decided we should go to some incredibly depressing exhibition, about how Jews have been hated over the years, just for being rich and powerful (pity we're not rich, although I suppose we are richer than lots of people, but that's not because we're Jewish, it's because Dad's parents gave him the money to buy a flat when he was twenty-one, so by the time he married Mum he could afford a house. According to him we are "asset rich and cash poor", although now Mum has her new job we are less cash poor than we were).

Lottie sounds interested – typically keen on educational stuff – and says someone at her school told her she should go to the Jewish Museum in Camden. I try and fail to imagine anyone at my school saying anything like that. Only Luke might… Luke…

Mum takes us to the museum, and then it turns out she's arranged to meet her friend Sarah there and have lunch after seeing the exhibition. Lottie says she has homework to do, and can she go home on the Tube, and I quickly say I want to do that too, and after a bit of dithering Mum agrees. "But you must call me to let me know you are safely home," she says. "There are a lot of nasty people around."

I dismiss this as typical Mum over-fussing, and I'm glad when she goes off to look at the exhibition with Sarah.

"Come on," says Lottie, but the last thing I want to do is look at some depressing museum. I'm depressed enough. "You go by yourself," I say. "I'm getting a snack."

She looks a bit surprised and (if I'm honest) a little disappointed, and for a minute I think I should change my mind, or at least ask if she wants to have a hot chocolate, but then I'd have to talk to her about Amina and Luke, and I'm not feeling ready for that.

There's a café just off the museum's foyer so I go in there for a comforting hot chocolate and croissant. I look at Amina's Insta feed knowing full well that I'm torturing myself. Sure enough, there are pictures of her and Luke, laughing in a park. Playing on the swings. Eating ice-cream.

Posing by graffiti on a wall.

I flick through his Twitter feed, which is mostly retweets from political accounts. Some of his retweets mention that we need to root out corruption. That there's a shadowy elite running the world who want to steal everything from poor people. He's so clever and he knows so much. It all makes my head hurt.

Did he prefer Amina to me because she's cleverer than me? Or maybe he never even noticed me at all? A big fat tear runs down my face and plops on to the croissant.

"Evie? Are you OK?"

It's Noah.

"Why are you here?" I demand.

He frowns. "Mum brought me to see the exhibition. Isn't that why you're here?"

"Yes. Lottie's upstairs. Our mums as well." I wait for him to go.

"I know, I saw her. I meant: why aren't you upstairs too?"

I make a face. "It's nothing to do with me, is it?"

"Nothing to do with you? Antisemitism?" His

eyes widen. "Evie, it's got everything to do with you."

There's something about his seriousness that reminds me of Luke. Tears pour down my cheeks. I try and hide them by taking a big gulp of hot chocolate, but start choking.

Noah hands me a serviette. "Look, I know it's upsetting..."

"It's really upsetting!" I wail. "I never even saw it coming!"

"These things – it feels like spring up out of nowhere," he says. "But it's all there, just waiting to happen."

I had no idea Noah knew so much about Luke and Amina.

"I never even realized!"

"That's why you should have gone round the exhibition," he says. "It explains where it all comes from."

Hang on, what?

"How can the exhibition explain why Amina and Luke are a couple now? What are you talking about?"

He blinks at me. "What are *you* talking about?"

"Amina and Luke! How did you know?"

"Oh…" He wrinkles his brow, as though trying to place him. "The idiot?"

I splutter. "How dare you?"

"Never mind. I thought you were upset about the whole Twitter thing."

"What Twitter thing?"

His mouth opens, and then his phone rings. He answers right away, listens intently and then says, "You got him? That's great. Where are you? OK, on the Northern Line, yes? OK. Maybe thirty minutes."

He ends the call. "I've got to go. See you Monday."

And he strides away, out of the front entrance of the museum.

I don't hesitate. I run after him, pushing through the crowds of tourists (normally I'd be totally distracted by Camden Market and all the stalls). Ahead of me I see him go into the Tube station. I go through the barriers, down the escalator.

Northern Line. But is he going north or south? I guess north – although which branch – to Edgware or to High Barnet – I have no idea.

I have no idea why I'm following him either. Only that I'm bored and sad and he's so mysterious. I want to see what he's doing.

Also – does he know something about Amina and Luke? And what is this Twitter thing he's on about?

As I get on to the platform I see Noah down the other end. The next train is High Barnet. I see him get on and I jump on too.

It's only when I sit down that I remember Mum and Lottie who I've left all alone in the museum. And there's no signal underground. But I send Lottie a text anyway. "Gone with Noah" I write. It's sort of true. "See you at home later." She'll get it once I get a signal.

It's crowded now, but as we travel further north, people get off, and by East Finchley when we come out from underground into the sunshine, the carriage is empty. At each station I stick my head out to try and spot Noah on the platform, but I don't. Maybe I missed him and he's got off already. I worry all the way to Woodside Park, where I see Noah walk past the window, and I leap out of the door before it closes. Luckily there are two women walking in front of me, and I'm pretty short so he doesn't see me.

I follow at a distance as he goes out of the station and down a leafy road. I keep to the other side of the road at a good distance. The road becomes less green and more grey, and it's looking slightly dodgier. I glance around, wondering exactly where I am, and when I look back, I realize that Noah is gone.

Vanished.

I stop and look all around, wondering where he went.

And then someone grabs me from behind.

CHAPTER NINETEEN

LOTTIE

Evie is in such a bad mood today. It's like she's fizzing and crackling with emotion. She's like a Coke can that's been shaken, and you know that as soon as you pull the tag all the foam will come gushing out, all over everything. She's been like this ever since she came back from school. But she won't talk about it. She's as unapproachable as Noah when he plugs in his music.

I'm stressed out too, about the tweets that Mum got. She got a lot of nice ones too, from people saying that Mum was quite right to speak out. But there were more nasty ones.

She said that Metro would deal with it all, and they'd told her to keep her head down because as the Voice of Nice, she'd gone outside her brief. "You just can't be nice all the time," she said. "I'm exhausted." Then she went to bed. The breakfast show is a killer.

I don't even know whether Evie knows about the tweets – she stayed in bed late and then wasn't up for talking. She was gloweringly furious, plugged into her headphones on the way to the museum.

Dad wanted to come with us. He tried to talk to Mum about the Twitter storm as well. But she really didn't want to discuss it, and he said he'd better try and meet his target for the week. I can see he's worrying about money. What if she loses this job? No one's saying it, but Dad and I are both thinking it, I can tell by the way he's frowning and the bags under his eyes. So I'm left with Angry Evie. At the museum I ask if she's OK. But she just gives me an unfriendly look which says, "Shut up, leave me alone."

Then she goes straight to the café. I don't

follow her. I want to see the exhibition. Even though it's about something that I know will be frightening and horrible.

There are photographs, paintings, newspaper articles and clips from news programmes. Some from the past, some from the present. The sort of stuff that Saffy and Topaz would say. Jews are rich. Jews are powerful. Jews can't be trusted.

Some of the pictures are so ugly that they make me want to cry. Some of them are just crazy. Some remind me of the pictures that I've studied in history lessons, learning about Nazi Germany. But some are much older. And some are from this year. They show me that the Nazi period was not unique at all. It drew on hundreds and hundreds of years of hatred.

One picture – a huge painting of ugly men in suits, playing chess on the backs of kneeling workers – was painted on a wall in east London, just a few years ago. East London. Not very far from where we live.

The exhibition explains how Jews were often banned from doing all sorts of jobs. How they were often forced into money lending. How some families became bankers – like one, the Rothschilds – and were then blamed for everything. Even now people say they rule the world and control all the banks. It's all lies.

Then I walk further into the museum and see the real Jews. Old men in turbans, selling dried rhubarb in the streets of London, hundreds of years ago. A "wheel of fortune" that was in a synagogue to help decide which families got help that week. I imagine being hungry and desperate, watching the wheel go round, waiting to find out if I'd get lucky and eat that night.

When I get to the café Evie isn't there any more. She must have gone round the exhibition after all. Mum and Sarah find me, and ask what I thought of the museum. "Are you all right, darling? You didn't find it too upsetting?" I reassure Mum that I'm fine, and no, I don't want to have lunch, and no, I haven't seen Noah or Evie, they must still be upstairs.

Then I drink chai tea and text Hannah and wait for Evie.

And just as I'm starting to worry that she's been kidnapped – *don't panic, Lottie* – I get a text. Something about going off with Noah.

I go home all by myself. Noah and Evie obviously couldn't be bothered to wait for me. I try not to mind. Just because we're sisters, just because we're twins, doesn't mean we have to be friends.

CHAPTER TWENTY

EVIE

I bite down hard on the hand over my mouth, and stamp my assailant's foot. Whoever has grabbed me yelps with pain and I spin round, keys in hand, ready to go for the eye.

It's Noah.

"Ow!" he gasps, holding his hand to his chest. "What are you doing?"

"What are *you* doing?" I hiss back, so relieved that I can't even be angry. "You grabbed me!"

"Shhh, I can explain," he says. "Come here and be quiet before you ruin everything."

He leads me behind a parked car where two

more boys in hoodies are crouched.

"Who are you?" one growls at me.

"Who are *you*?" I whisper back, but the second one, the taller one, pulls up a mask to cover his face, and that's when I see that he has a pot of paint and a brush. He picks it up and moves out behind the car. There's no one around. He moves very fast, over the road to a blue front door, and dips a brush into the paint.

"What—" I start, but Noah scowls at me, and I realize that now is not the time for questions.

The paint is red as blood.

Moving quickly, the tall boy starts writing on the front door, big letters.

NAZI.

Then, on the white wall:

BIGOT.

And finally, on the black car parked in the driveway, a swastika. Noah's watching, eyes intent. The boy next to me (freckles, small dark eyes) is keeping watch in the other direction. Suddenly I notice the movement behind one of the windows of the house with the red door.

"Run!" Noah yells. The front door opens and a man – just an ordinary man, mid height, middle aged – lets out a bellow of fury. The painter throws the last of his paint straight at him and runs. None of us wait to see what happens. Noah grabs my hand and we run and run, dodging around corners, over driveways and in and out of front gardens, until we come to a halt at the back of a derelict pub. I don't know where the others go. I'm breathing so hard I can't catch my breath. *This is what it feels like to be Lottie*, I think.

In the distance we can hear the wail of police sirens. Noah sinks to the ground, his back against the pub wall. I follow. We both need to get our breath back.

"You followed me, didn't you?" he says eventually. "Why?"

"Because you just ran away from me mid-sentence! So rude!"

He shrugs. "I'm sorry. I got the call. The timing was urgent."

"What, for you to go and graffiti a house?"

"You're a child. You won't understand."

Talk about pompous.

"I'm fourteen years old," I snap. "You're only, what, fifteen?"

"Nearly sixteen," he says.

I roll my eyes. "I mean, you're right. You're the adult and I'm a child."

"You have a point," he says and smiles. His smile is kind of cute and dimpled, I guess, but you don't get round me with a cute smile.

"Who *were* those guys? And what were you doing?"

"I can't tell you too much," he says. "I don't want you telling the police. Or your parents, Eva."

"*Evie!*"

"Evie. I think it's safer the less I tell you."

"OK, Captain America," I say. "You don't have to tell me anything. You and your bunch of superheroes. Let me guess. You can just nod."

His eyes are narrow. "OK," he says cautiously.

"You guys are like vigilantes," I say. "You track down racists." I think for a moment. "They're online trolls and somehow you work out their addresses."

A slight nod.

"And then you go and graffiti their houses so everyone knows what they are."

He shrugs. "More or less. Fight back against the haters. Make them feel scared."

"But how did you get involved from *Paris*? Wait, did you do this sort of thing there and get in trouble? And *that's* why you had to leave?"

"Not quite," he says, smiling faintly. "OK, I'll tell you. But you must promise not to tell anyone."

"I swear," I say, "I'd rather *die*," I add for emphasis, as though I really mean it.

I know differently now.

CHAPTER TWENTY-ONE

LOTTIE

I go home, all on my own, images from the exhibition whirling around my head. Cartoons with hook-nosed men counting their money. I think about the couple from the Kindertransport who came to our school. How can people still lie about what happened, when the facts – the truth – is right there?

And then I think about Saffy, and how she's not said a word to me since that day (Miss Klein warned her off, I suspect), but I still shrivel up inside when I see her cold, blue glare from across the classroom.

It makes me feel angry. And feeling angry is better than feeling anxious. It's energizing. Feeling anxious is like drowning. Anger is heat, it's fire.

I once read that anxiety is just anger pushed down inside. Two sides of the same coin. Angry people are often anxious, frightened people, and anxious people are secretly angry. They don't even realize it.

When I get home, I text Evie, "Where are you?" but there's no reply. She's probably doing something fun with Noah.

Dad's still out. Mum's having lunch with Sarah. I wish someone was here, so I could discuss the exhibition and what Mum said on the radio, and the tweets, and everything that's whirling round my head.

I make some toast and hummus and try not to worry about Evie. I try her phone again. Nothing.

I should do homework, so I log into my laptop. But then I open up Twitter.

They've got even worse. They've got a lot

worse. I read words like *whore, slut, bitch, kill* and *rape. The Holocaust DIDN'T happen. You bought Billy Martin's job with your Jewish money. Go gas yourself like your relatives. The Jews deserve what they get Hahahahaha.*

And then the *what abouts.*

What about Israel?

What about Palestine?

Hypocrite.

Jew.

Liar.

I can feel the anger rising up in me again. A bit of shame in there too, like that day in the canteen. And before I know what I'm doing, I'm logging on to Mum's account. Someone has to stand up to these bullies. They're worse even than Saffy and co because they're completely anonymous. Well, I won't stand for it. What was her password? Evie?08.

You're a bunch of spineless bigots. Leave me and my family alone. I'm proud of being Jewish and I stand by everything I said. It's called being brave. You wouldn't know the meaning of the word.

And it feels good to be answering back, to be telling them what they are. I don't feel like Anxious Lottie at all. I feel strong and brave. Like I imagine Evie feels all the time.

I must try this more often.

CHAPTER TWENTY-TWO

EVIE

It's cold and smelly by the side of the derelict pub, and the ground is full of litter, the sort of litter you never should get near to: syringes and – yuck – condoms. So we cautiously walk down the road, and find a café, the sort my Dad calls a "greasy spoon" although actually everything is spotlessly clean, gleaming under strip lighting. Noah orders coffee and I have my second hot chocolate of the day.

"Go on then," I say.

He takes a deep breath. "Before we moved to Paris, I lived in north London," he says. "I was a typical little Jewish boy. I went to a Jewish school. I went to the synagogue. All my friends were mostly Jewish. I lived in the bubble.

"And then, when I was seven, we went to live in Paris. My dad's French, and he always wanted to go back there, and then he got a job. Mum said it would be exciting. I'd learn another language, make new friends, all that stuff.

"Anyway, I went to a French-Jewish school and people were friendly. It was a bit hard at first, but once I had the language down…" He smiles. "I was pleased with myself. I felt very confident. I imagined travelling the world like this, learning new languages – it was my dream."

"Isn't it still?" I ask.

"Not any more." His face goes hard. He seems too young to have lost his dreams. Mine are all that keep me going sometimes. Dreams of becoming a comedy star, going on the stage and making people laugh. I couldn't bear to lose that hope.

"There was an attack on a Jewish school in Toulouse. I don't know if you heard about it on the news." I shake my head.

He hates talking about it, I can tell. "Toulouse is in the south of France. A long way from Paris. And there was –" he swallows – "a shooter. He said Jews were responsible for deaths in Palestine. He killed people, children too. And my parents, they tried to keep it from us but … you know how it is. You hear bits and pieces. But not the whole story, and that makes it worse, somehow."

I think back to when Dad lost his job. They didn't tell Lottie and me for ages. All we had to go on were scraps of overheard conversations, a feeling that something was terribly wrong. It was scarier than the truth.

"Anyway," he goes on, "I started noticing other stuff after that. My friend, Davide, he lived in an estate, you'd call it here, and some people had it in for him. It was nasty stuff. In the end his family moved to Israel. Lots of people did.

"And then there were the *Charlie Hebdo* attacks." He glances at me. "You'll remember *that*?"

"*Charlie Hebdo* is a magazine?" I say uncertainly.

"Yes, one that specializes in saying the unsayable. Jokes that push the limits. Someone was so offended by one of the jokes, they broke in and shot people."

Killed for making jokes.

"And then a few days later, another attack. He went to a Jewish shop. Killed people whose only crime was to go shopping for food. Kosher food. My mum goes there all the time. But she wasn't there that day. I was at school at the time. Just around the corner. We all had to hide away while it was happening… I'll never forget it. My teacher was crying. And then later, we found out … the terrorist, his real target wasn't the shop. It was *us*. Little Jewish kids in a Jewish school."

I feel a bit sick. At primary school, my biggest worry was whether my best friend would dump me. (She did, all the time. Amina is a way better friend.) Hiding in your classroom, thinking you might be killed – that's what happens in America. Not here. Not in Europe.

"Yeah, so that really woke me up. I knew that some people hated Jews. Really hated them.

That shooter was Muslim—"

"My best friend is Muslim," I interject, bristling. "She'd never ever hurt anyone because they were Jewish."

"Of course not. Some people who hate Jews are Muslim, some are Neo-Nazis, some are white supremacists, some are left wingers. You don't need to look far to find people who hate Jews."

I shiver. The impression I'd got was that people had stopped hating Jews after the Second World War. That people realized it wasn't a good idea. Anyway, maybe time to stop talking about horrible things happening in France and cut to Noah going all vigilante on the streets of London.

"How do you track these people down?" I say. "These trolls?"

"I've known these guys for years, from summer camp. We hack accounts. Find their address. And then we pay them a visit and we let everyone know what they are. That they can't hide online for ever. It's not like the social media companies are going to do anything about it, so we will."

I can see, from his point of view it's all really

straightforward, and satisfying, and right. Street justice, as doled out by Noah and his mates. And yet: "And you always get the right people? Because if you got the wrong guy that could be terrible."

He nods. "I know," he says quietly. "It is not perfect. But at least we're doing *something*." He hesitates. "Something happened, before I left Paris. A guy tried to knock my kippah off my head on the way to shul and I fought back." He sees me looking blank and laughs.

"You mean like temple?"

"That's what the Americans call it, yup."

"Oh, OK." I don't like to admit that I really only know about Jewish stuff from American TV.

"Anyway, I got hurt. I think it was the final straw for Mum."

"So now you're in London."

"Mum wants to stay in London. But Dad and I, we think if we're leaving France, we should go to Israel. That's the only place we can really be safe."

We're silent for a bit. I wonder what time it is. My phone is dead so I can't check.

Then he says: "You do stand-up, don't you?"

"Yeah," I say. I'm pleased that he knows.

"Do you know any Jewish jokes?"

"I don't think so."

"I'm going to tell you a Jewish joke," he says. "Two Jews, Moshe and Itzik, are walking in the forest." Weird names I think, but don't say – there's nothing worse than having a joke interrupted. "And they see two men coming towards them. Moshe panics, turns to Itzik and says: "We're done for! There are two of them and we're all alone!"

I laugh, because this is clearly the punchline, but I'm not sure I get it. There are two against two, right? And how does Moshe know the men want to hurt them?

"I don't get it," I confess.

"The point is," Noah says, "that, even when we're together, we always feel alone. That anyone who isn't Jewish might turn on us. We've had centuries of being persecuted. Well, I've had enough of that. I'm never going to give up fighting back. Whatever it takes."

CHAPTER TWENTY-THREE

LOTTIE

I haven't moved. I sit there, phone in hand. And I watch the notifications explode.

The hashtag #NicetoNasty springs up and then grows and grows. It's trending.

They wanted Mum to notice them, I realize. I gave them what they wanted. I try and call Hannah, but then I remember she doesn't use her phone on a Saturday. I try and do some homework but I can't concentrate. I'm too scared to call Mum.

Eventually Evie comes home. She hardly apologizes for leaving me all alone at the museum, and bounces off to do whatever Evie does in her room. Then Dad gets back, yawning. He asks me what I thought of the exhibition. I tell him it was very interesting, but he falls asleep in an armchair before I can add that it was also scary and upsetting. And that I've gone and done something really potentially stupid. And then Mum comes back.

She doesn't say anything to me, just shakes Dad awake. They go into the kitchen and talk. And then she calls me in and Evie down from her room.

Mum is sitting at the kitchen table, her hands gripped together. Dad is rubbing her back. Evie comes shuffling in, looking grouchy.

"What do you girls know about computer hackers?"

"I—" I start, but Evie interrupts.

"Nothing. Absolutely nothing. Don't know any, have no interest in any, haven't really heard anything about them."

Mum's looking as serious as I've ever seen her. "Someone hacked into my Twitter account today, and—"

"It was me," I say, so fast that I can't stop to think if confessing is a good idea or not. "I did it. I'm sorry I didn't hack your account – I remembered the password."

Mum and Dad stare at me. So does Evie. I can't tell if her mouth is open because she's horrified or impressed.

"Why, Lottie?" Mum says, very gently.

"Yes, why?" says Evie, not gently at all.

"I couldn't bear it," I say. "All those people saying those disgusting things and no one saying anything back."

"What disgusting things?" says Evie.

"Oh, Lottie," says Mum. "I know how you feel. But the advice from Metro's social media people was to keep my head down and don't feed the trolls. That's what they want, and this doesn't achieve anything."

She doesn't seem angry, just exhausted and worried. That's worse.

Evie is scanning Mum's Twitter notifications and her eyes are wide and amazed. "Oh my God!

How is it legal to say things like this?"

"Like what?" I choke out – I haven't dared look at Twitter for hours.

"Like – oh, never mind. People are horrible." She looks a bit sick. "And you sort of encouraged them, Lottie?"

"It's not legal," says Mum. "The threats are illegal. Metro have called in the police. And Lottie didn't mean to spark it off again…"

"Well," says Dad, slowly. "You're braver than I thought, little Lottie mouse."

"Don't call me that!" That was his name for me when I was tiny and had all sorts of health problems from being premature, and had to go into hospital for weeks because the tiniest cold could affect my lungs. But now I'm taller than Evie!

Evie huffs. I'd forgotten she was in a terrible bad mood.

"If I'd done something like this, you wouldn't be saying I was brave! You'd be saying I had to give up my phone, or my laptop, or be grounded or something. Typical! It's so unfair!"

"No, we wouldn't," says Mum,

"You totally would." She glares at Mum. "Why did you have to start all this in the first place? You had one job! Literally *being* nice! Now people will think you are … political. They'll think all kinds of things."

"Like what?" asks Dad.

"You've just gone and stuck a label on us. We're not victims, all that stuff isn't such a big deal and it doesn't happen here. I don't even want to be Jewish. I don't know what it means."

Mum bites her lip.

"Evie, it *is* a big deal. And it does happen here. And you are Jewish."

"What? You never wanted to be Jewish until it suited you!" And Evie storms out of the room, and into the living room, where she puts on the TV, very loud, sending gales of audience laughter into the kitchen.

"She's upset," I say. "She's been in a bad mood all day. Something is bothering her."

Mum looks at her hands. "I never realized," she says softly. "I never realized what I was doing wrong. I didn't want to burden you with the past. But I should have realized you can't leave it behind."

We sit in awkward silence. I'm wondering what I can say to make Mum stop looking so sad and Dad so worried. It's all my fault, even though they are being nice about it. And then there's a crash from next door. The sound of breaking glass. And Evie screams.

CHAPTER TWENTY-FOUR

EVIE

It happens so fast. One minute I'm watching TV, minding my own business; the next I hear a crash and something hits the side of my head. McGonagall flees from the room as though he's being chased by a truckload of demons.

I put my hand to my cheek and when I pull it away there's blood.

Something loud and terrified and screaming comes out of my mouth. Mum and Dad and Lottie come running into the room and Mum grabs me into a hug.

"Evie!"

"Lottie, get the first aid box! And some water and kitchen roll... Let me see, Evie."

I take my hand away and she dabs at my cheek with wet kitchen roll and says, "It's OK, just a scratch."

Dad's on the phone. "Yes ... someone threw a brick ... front bay ... just now... No, I didn't see anything." His voice breaks. "It hit my daughter. Yeah, OK. Thank you."

A brick! And then I see it, lying on the floor. A huge brick, lying among shards of glass. I guess one of them hit me. If the brick had whacked me in the face – or one of the sharp splinters had ripped into my neck... Just thinking about it makes me feel sick and dizzy, as though I'm going to pass out.

Mum holds a cloth to my face until it stops bleeding, then puts on antiseptic cream and a plaster. I can't stop shaking. Mum's hand is unsteady too.

"The police are coming," says Dad. He holds out his arms and I collapse against him, grateful for the comfortable Dad-ness of his old jumper to cry into. He rubs my head. "There, there. It's OK. Tell us what happened."

I can't get the words out. I try to say "a brick came though the window", but my voice – my big, loud, comedy voice – seems to have disappeared. I can't even squeak.

I could have been badly hurt. This is the most dramatic thing that's ever happened to me. There must be material I can use. *Did you hear the one about the girl who was sitting watching TV and a brick smacked her in the head?* It's scary, but there has to be a funny side. There has to be. There always is.

I just can't think what it is right now.

Mum makes me a cup of tea with two sugars ("for shock", she says) and it's disgusting, so Lottie makes me hot chocolate and Dad gets her to pour in a little bit of rum. "My mum swore by it for her nerves," he says. That's disgusting too, but not as bad.

"I should call Sarah," says Mum suddenly. "She might not want Noah staying any more if…"

Noah. It can't be a coincidence, can it? I was

with them, when they attacked that guy's house. What if he tracked us, followed me on to the Tube and to my front door. Found a brick and took his revenge.

Should I tell someone? Or course I should. But I want to talk to Noah first.

Lottie comes in then. She's holding the brick. There are three letters painted on it, in black.

J-E-W. Jew.

CHAPTER TWENTY-FIVE

LOTTIE

Everyone tells me it's not my fault. Mum, Dad, the police. Even Evie says I shouldn't feel guilty.

"If anyone started this, it's Mum," she says. "And it might be nothing to do with her anyway."

She looks worried though, which isn't like her.

Noah's staying in north London, on his grandma's sofa for now, and coming here to south London every day for school. He comes round on Monday after school with some flowers for Mum.

"It's all my fault," I tell him. "I sent that tweet."

"It's no one's fault but the person who threw the brick," he says. "Not yours, not your mum's. Theirs." But he looks worried too.

Hannah says pretty much the same when I tell her. "Lots of people admire your mum, you know," she says. She's rooting through her bag for her science book. "Listen, do you want to come to dinner at my house Friday night?"

I tell her I would love to. But for some reason I don't want to tell Mum and Dad. Instead I make up a tennis tournament, and pretend I am going to Saffy's house, and Dad says he'll pick me up at ten p.m., so I have to think of a reason why it's not actually Saffy's house but someone else's. And I can't really justify to myself why I'm lying about it, but on the Thursday night, I'm lying in bed kind of excited, kind of nervous, and I realize that I'm avoiding telling people about Hannah just in case Mum doesn't want me to get "too" Jewish. It might worry her even more.

And also, Mum and Dad love it that I play tennis, because it means I'm healthy and fit, not asthmatic and ill. And I don't want to tell them what happened with Saffy. It will just be more fuss, and that's the last thing we need right now.

When we get to Hannah's house, it reminds me of Christmas a bit – no decorations, but an amazing smell of fresh bread and roast potatoes, and Dalya is laying the dining table, which is covered with a snow white tablecloth. We help her – "just twelve of us tonight" – says Hannah, counting on her fingers. Hannah's mum – "Do call me Shira" – is short, like Hannah, and wears a scarf that covers her hair. She's got big eyes and a big smile, and she's easy to feel at home with.

She says to me, "I hear your mother is Bex Harris from Metropolitan Radio."

"Yes," I say.

"Well, please tell her that I love her show and I admire what she's doing. There's so much snark and nastiness these days. We need someone doing something positive."

"The voice of nice," I say.

"Exactly! And she's been so brave, speaking up for all of us."

I want to explain how horrible it has been and

how I made it worse, but there's a huge lump in my throat.

"Are you OK?" asks Hannah's mum, very gently. "Has it been difficult?"

"It has a bit," I whisper.

"Remember the vast majority of people don't go screaming on to social media, sharing every nasty thought in their heads. I know it's hard to believe, but it's true."

Her voice is so gentle and kind that before I know it, I am telling them about the brick too.

"But that's terrifying," says Shira. "Awful! Are you all right?"

"I don't know how they knew where we live," I say.

"That's so frightening!" says Dalya. Her eyes are huge in her face. "Could it happen to us, Mum?"

"Because our mum is such a celebrity?" says Hannah. "Don't make it all about you, Dalya."

"It's about all of us," says Shira, sitting down at the table. "It's about being Jewish, and being different. Bullies will always want to hurt us. But try not to be scared. We have lots of people to look after us."

"How can I not be scared?" says Dalya.

"You just get on with it," says Hannah, lifting her chin. "Like you get on the Tube, knowing a bomb could go off. You cross the road, knowing you could get hit by a car. Walk home, knowing you could get mugged."

"That's enough, Hannah," says Shira.

"It's about probability," I say. "We have to weigh up the odds against something awful happening, or we won't do anything at all." And right now I feel as though my personal odds have changed. Now that one terrible thing has happened, the door is open for everything else.

"None of this is new," says Shira. "All through history, Jewish people have had these worries. And yet, somehow, here we are." She looks at the clock. "And it's nearly time for candle-lighting. Let's finish laying the table."

On to the table goes cutlery for twelve people, glasses, and two plaited loaves of bread, dotted with sesame seeds, covered with an embroidered cloth. Hannah pours wine into little glass goblets.

"It's time!" says Hannah's mum, and I see that there's a tray on the sideboard with three pairs of candlesticks, all ready with white candles.

"I assumed you'd want to light your own, Lottie," she says. "Dalya, you've only got a few weeks to wait."

"I've never done it before." I'm nervous.

"Don't worry, just copy us." We light our candles, then all three move our hands in circles, then cover our eyes. They say the Hebrew words slowly, and I follow them.

"All we are saying is that God is blessed for commanding us to light the Sabbath lights," Hannah explains.

Shira says "Shabbat shalom" and kisses both her daughters. "Don't worry, Lottie, I won't embarrass my daughter by kissing you … but Shabbat shalom and welcome to our house."

"Welcome to the Friday night experience," says Hannah, laughing.

I'm bursting with questions. "What was that thing we did with our arms?" I ask, worried that

I've asked something so basic and obvious that they'll laugh.

"We're welcoming in the Sabbath," says Hannah.

"Like she was a queen," says Dalya.

"Or a bride," says Hannah's mother.

Hannah's dad and her brothers arrive from the synagogue, all of them big and tall, and their friends, Dalya's friend Poppy and her parents. There are prayers before the meal, and we all have a sip of wine and a piece of the plaited bread, which is sweet and chewy.

First we have chicken soup, with carrots and pasta in it, and then roast chicken and potatoes, an aubergine stuffed with vegetable rice for the vegetarians, and about five different sorts of vegetables. I wonder if they have so much food every week. It's delicious anyway. And no one is watching me, or worrying about me, or checking if I'm eating, so I do.

When dessert is served (apple crumble, mango sorbet) Hannah's dad says it's time to go around the table sharing something good that's happened during the week, and something we're looking forward to in the week ahead.

I panic for a moment at the thought of everyone listening to me, everyone looking at me, but it feels so natural and normal in their house, that I manage it. Even though my "something good" was getting an A for my English essay, and the thing I'm looking forward to is getting my biology test over with, which is really feeble.

I listen to the little glimpses of other people's lives. Poppy is planning to make an alternative version of the London Underground map for her friend's batmitzvah. "The Northern Line is going to be all her friends' names, and the Victoria Line all the music she likes, but we haven't decided what the Central Line is yet." Hannah's brother Joe's band is getting a gig at his college. And I realize that there are all sorts of different ways of living that are nothing to do with school or exams or homework.

At the end of the meal, they pass out little booklets. Mine has Hannah's name on the front, and she explains that the books have prayers they say after a meal, and this booklet was printed for her batmitzvah.

"What are the prayers?" I ask.

"Oh, we just say thank you to God for everything."

"When you've been persecuted for years, you don't take anything for granted," says Hannah's dad, who looks a lot like Hannah, except he has a ginger beard and a bald patch. "Every little thing – just sitting around a table, eating with the family, we express our gratitude. We're celebrating everyday life, all the time."

"It doesn't always *feel* like celebrating," says Hannah. "Not when you're the one stuck in the kitchen getting it all ready."

"There she goes again," mutters one of her brothers.

"It's all right for you, you're not treated like a second-class citizen."

"Oh, shut up, Hannah."

Before Hannah can reply, her dad clears his throat and starts singing. They all join in, and sing in harmony, even though Hannah and her brother are making faces at each other across the table. I try and follow the English translation, but after a bit just let the music wash over me.

Afterwards, we all help clear up. And then my phone starts vibrating in my pocket. It must be Dad, here to pick me up.

"I'd better go," I say. "My dad's waiting for me."

"Do come again," says Shira. "Shabbat shalom."

"I will," I say. "Thank you. Shabbat shalom."

Walking out of their house into the cold, walking down the path, I have a strange sensation. I'm going back to my family, but instead of going home, I'm walking away from where I want to be.

"Did you win?" asks Dad when I get into the car, and I feel bad. I think how nice it is that he came all this way to pick me up, and how much I love him. And here I am lying to him. But I'm not quite ready to tell him where I was. "I did," I say. "It was great."

CHAPTER TWENTY-SIX

EVIE

"That's terrible," says Amina. "Awful. Why would someone throw a brick through your window?"

"I have no idea," I lie.

"Were the police helpful?" she asks.

That's a hard question to answer. They were definitely very nice. They asked loads of questions. They offered us a Hate Crime Support Officer. They were very interested in the tweets to Mum's account and said they'd go through and look for any threats of violence.

But there are no witnesses and no forensic evidence on the actual brick. So it's down to

CCTV evidence, if they can find any. I didn't tell them about Noah. I want to talk to him first.

"They were nice," I say, and then immediately feel bad. Of course the police were nice to us. We're white and middle class, and exactly the sort of people the police are nice to. It'd probably be different if we looked more like Amina.

"Do you think it's anything to do with all that stuff on Twitter about your mum?"

We haven't really discussed any of that, and I realize that I'm a bit nervous about it. People seem so worked up about all kinds of stuff, particularly Israel and Palestine, and although Mum and Dad have tried to talk me through massive history lessons stretching back in time to before the Roman Empire, I have no real idea what I think about it, let alone what Amina and her family might say.

Some people seem to assume that a really complicated situation is a matter of taking one side or another. The Jewish side, or the Muslim side. And although it feels crazy that my best friend and I could fall out over the politics of a place thousands of miles away, crazy things can happen.

"I don't know anything about all that stuff," I say. "It's Mum's business, not mine."

"Yes, but it's really important stuff," she says. "My dad says—"

I cut her off. "I don't want to talk about it."

She raises her eyebrows. "Oh. OK. If you say so. Well, I said I'd meet Luke. Do you want to come?"

I'd virtually forgotten about Luke. But now all the heartbreak comes flooding back.

"No. I don't think so. I'll see you later."

She hesitates for a micro-second, and then says, "OK, see you," and disappears into the lunchtime crowd.

I love Amina. She's my friend. We watch TV together, and do each other's make-up, and share memes on Snapchat. We invent dances for TikTok. We eat popcorn.

Why do I feel awkward and guilty when I talk to my friend about what happened to me? Why can't I explain that to her?

What am I so scared of?

CHAPTER TWENTY-SEVEN

LOTTIE

I am dressed in sequins and gold. I have a tiara and a red wig, tumbling past my shoulders. Hannah is applying dark, glittery make-up to my eyes.

"Look up," she says, and I feel the brush of a mascara stick. "Perfect," she says. "Queen Esther."

I twirl around, feeling the long skirt against my legs. It's a shimmery heavy silk. It used to belong to Hannah's mum, and she's lent it to me for tonight. It's the Jewish festival of Purim and apparently, fancy dress is the thing.

Hannah is dressed as a rabbit, in a furry

onesie. I asked her if she wouldn't prefer to dress as the queen, and she said no, she'd been Queen Esther for years and years when she was a kid and now she likes to mix things up a bit.

I prefer my sparkly dress. But I like her rabbit onesie too. It suits her.

"OK, now pick your weapon."

She holds out a wicker basket full of instruments. I pick some castanets. She takes a tambourine.

"Remind me what all this is about," I say, suddenly feeling a bit nervous.

"Oh, wait and see, it's nothing like normal shul, way more fun. Everyone dresses up, don't worry."

I know this is true because at lunch some of the girls on our table were talking about their costumes. It still feels strange to be wearing fancy dress to go to a synagogue. Especially for the first time!

"OK, Purim 101," says Hannah. "We are celebrating because Queen Esther – that's you – saved all the Jews in the Persian Empire from being killed by Hamam, the king's evil advisor. The story – or megillah – is going to be read in shul this evening, by ... ta-da ... by me." She bows. "Not just me, lots of the women. I'm just doing a little bit. We're in a side room, obviously, while the patriarchy have the main synagogue. And afterwards everyone parties and celebrates. Classic Jewish festival: they tried to kill us, they failed, now eat."

"Tell me more about Queen Esther," I say, staring at myself in the mirror. Is that really me, all glitter and dark eyes?

"She did well in difficult circumstances," says Hannah, "although she had to marry some sexist pig of a king in order to save my people. My favourite queen in the whole story is Vashti, the first wife. She stood up to the patriarchy. A real feminist heroine. But don't worry, you can read the whole story in shul."

We go downstairs and show off our costumes. Dalya is a Disney princess. One brother is a penguin and the other has his football kit on. And Shira is wearing a dark trouser suit.

"Looking good, Mum," says Hannah.

Shira adds a black coat and a wide-brimmed hat – which makes her look exactly like the sort of Jews I've seen on television, or in our RE book. "Ultra Orthodox Jews", they call them.

"Now, where did I put my beard?" she says.

"I can't believe it's Lottie's first time in a synagogue," says Hannah, embarrassed, but her mum just smiles and says, "Don't judge it on today, Lottie, it's not exactly typical."

"It's more fun than usual," says Hannah, "and more equal. Usually the women just get to watch…"

"Oh, that's not exactly fair," says her mum. "We do have women's services. And women have their own role—"

"At home!" says Hannah, scornfully.

"And we can study – even be rabbis."

"That's so cool," I say.

"Thank you, Lottie. Hannah thinks we should join a more progressive arm of Judaism, and I can see why – but I prefer the tradition I grew up in. And I find that when women push to do more,

178

there are ways. As you will see today."

All of this talk, all this new information, makes me feel connected to something – something bigger and more important than me. Evie would probably say I was joining a cult. But it doesn't feel like that. It feels right.

At the synagogue, I'm surprised to see there are security guards outside. They recognize Hannah's parents and let us in, and her dad and brother go into the main synagogue, while all the women crowd into a smaller side room.

I don't understand everything that's going on. But I read the story in English from the book Hannah gives me, as the women go up one by one and sing bits of it in Hebrew.

If I close my eyes I can almost see them. Arrogant King Ahasuerus, thin-lipped, with oiled hair and beard, having a seven day party at his palace, lounging on couches of silver and gold, under blue and white awnings hung on silver rods and marble columns; on a pavement of green, white, shell, and onyx, knocking back wine from golden goblets.

He calls for his wife Vashti to dance at his party, although she's holding her own banquet for the women of the palace. I can almost hear the jeers of the drunken men, and feel angry on Vashti's behalf. She refuses.

The king worries that if word got out that Vashti said no to his party all the wives in his kingdom would revolt against their husbands, so he sends word around the kingdom that Vashti is no longer queen. He's looking for a new one. The process for finding a new queen is like a beauty contest for the whole kingdom, and it makes it clear that women in the palace are treated like slaves – or people in a reality TV show – treated with perfumes and ointments, until they are ready to be presented to the king.

And the king loves Esther more than all the women, and he places the royal crown on her head and makes her queen instead of Vashti – but he keeps some other maidens in the palace as well. And all this time Esther is keeping a huge secret – that she's Jewish. Her Uncle Mordecai has told her not to tell anyone.

Then – enter the villain – Haman. As soon as his name is mentioned, all the women around me make a noise, with the instruments they've brought with them, some stamping their feet as well.

Haman is upset because Mordecai won't bow to him and gets the king to agree that he can kill all the Jews in the kingdom, "both young and old, little children and women". I think of the school assembly, of Hitler's campaign of destruction against a people. It's time to make a noise again and this time I join in, stamping my feet and shaking the castanets, and I'm surprised to find that it does make me feel stronger and braver.

It's almost enough to make me forget the sickening thud of that brick coming through the window.

If I were Esther, I'd have gone running straight to the king and told him that Haman needed to be stopped. But Esther – after talking to her uncle – does things much more cautiously. She and her maidens fast for three days. Then she goes to the king, and he points his golden sceptre at her, and asks what she wants.

Esther asks the king and Haman to a banquet. And then another one. All this time Haman is getting ready to hang the Jews from an enormous gallows.

And at last, Esther is brave enough to explain to the king that Haman – evil Haman – is going to kill her and her people. The king is so angry that he leaves the feast and goes out into the orchard – and while he does it, Haman begs Esther for his life, drunkenly falling on to her couch. Of course the king comes rushing back in, and jumps to conclusions. And I think about the #metoo movement, and the women abused by powerful men, and I see it's been going on for thousands of years.

The king sees through Haman, and orders that he should be killed. Esther falls at his feet and begs for him to send a letter – sealed with his ring – to stop the Jews being killed. And the letters go out, carried by men on horses and camels, to 127 provinces of the Persian empire. Mordecai,

Esther's uncle, was given Haman's house, and a huge golden crown and "the Jews had light and joy, and gladness and honour."

But the ending of the book scares me – it's about the way the Jews then fought the people who wanted to kill them, the enemies and the haters. Seventy-five thousand people died, said the story. So I'm also thinking about the way that fear and relief can end badly, that peace doesn't necessarily come with victory. And I wonder how Queen Esther felt about all those deaths, and her drunken husband's lazy use of his power, after this all ended. Then the story is over, and there's a party with sort of folk dancing, and I forget all these deep thoughts while I whirl and hop and try and follow the instructions. And I feel almost part of all this noise and celebration and fun.

Afterwards we go back to Hannah's house and eat triangular cakes stuffed with different fillings – hamantaschen, they are called, Haman's ears – and Shira asks me what I thought of it.

"I liked it," I say. "It's just – all those people died at the end. Because one man was jealous."

"Yes," she says, "it is very troubling. And maybe it can be seen as a warning. Petty revenge can escalate out of control."

"But we celebrate anyway?" I say. *We.* I've said it without realizing.

"When you're an oppressed people, you take every opportunity to celebrate victory over the oppressor. Even if it's bloody and compromised and imperfect. It's a reminder that we should not forget. No one is perfect. Not us Jews. Only God."

CHAPTER TWENTY-EIGHT

EVIE

Typical! If it had been me who'd commandeered Mum's verified Twitter feed with ten thousand followers and massively escalated a hate attack, then I'd have been punished for years and years. Grounded. No pocket money. Netflix privileges removed. Phone crushed beneath the wheels of Dad's Uber. That sort of thing. But when it comes to golden child Lottie – nothing. If anything, Mum and Dad seem almost proud of her.

Although … maybe the brick wasn't Lottie's fault at all. Maybe it was all down to Noah, and me.

They even let Lottie stay overnight at her friend Saffy's for a tennis tournament. Although it must be a funny sort of tennis tournament if they didn't have to bring a racket. (OK, I'm nosy – I checked and Lottie's was still in her cupboard. What on earth is she up to?)

Anyway, never mind Lottie; despite the police saying that they are doing everything they can, the person who tried to kill me by throwing the brick through the window is still at large. I need to talk to Noah, but it's more difficult now he's not staying with us.

In the end I manage to track him down in the school library.

"I need to talk to you," I hiss, trying to ignore the cluster of Year Nine girls huddled around the self-help section, blatantly staring at us.

"What is it? I have work to do," he says, not taking his eyes off the computer screen.

"I don't care!" I drop my voice to a whisper. "Have you thought that maybe that brick attack had nothing to do with Lottie's tweet? That maybe it was a revenge attack aimed at *you*?"

"Shhh." Noah looks around. "Not here. I'll meet you after school, OK? At McDonalds?"

So, three hours later, here we are. In a booth. He's looking impossibly cool, having shed his uniform and put on a leather jacket and jeans at some point between school and here. (Who does that? And where?) I'm looking impossibly uncool in blazer and brown kilt. We aren't allowed to wear trousers and the kilts are an unflattering mid-calf length, meaning that for a short person like me the look is more medieval peasant or monk. In the meantime, Lottie goes to her all-girls school in black trousers, black blazer, white shirt and a black and red tie, looking like she runs the London police service.

"Go on then," I say. "Start talking."

"It can't be because of us," Noah says. "There is no way they could have tracked me."

"Bit of a coincidence though, isn't it? You come to London, set yourself up as troll hunter in chief … and suddenly we get bricks flying through the window!"

"It is just that, a coincidence," he insists. "The

brick, it's because your mum is on the radio. She gets the attention of some unpleasant people and … there you go."

I sit back. "Whatever happened, Lottie made things worse sending that tweet. She's so stupid!"

He frowns. "I think Lottie was brave to send that tweet. It takes guts to stand up to these people. And the police are taking it all seriously, they'll find whoever it is. It's better here than France, Mum says."

"Yeah," I say, "and you know what else they'll take seriously? You guys painting 'bigot' on someone's front door. Aren't you just as bad as whoever threw that brick?"

Noah's face is set and furious.

"Look, I don't need some kid telling me what to do. I didn't ask you to follow me. You nearly jeopardized the whole operation."

"You're not in the army, Noah! You're a fifteen-year-old prat who is breaking the law!"

We're both glaring at each other when suddenly I hear Amina's voice. "Hey! Evie!"

She's standing right in front of me, and so is

Luke Braybourne. They're both clutching piles of leaflets. Luke is wearing a padded jacket, but Amina just has her school blazer. She looks freezing.

"Hey," I say, unenthusiastically. "What're you up to, guys?" I brace myself for tales of romance and excitement.

"Handing out these leaflets," says Luke.

"And now we're having a break," says Amina. "I am starving!" She squeezes in next to me. Reluctantly, Noah moves along to let Luke sit next to him. They've got fries and milkshakes. My mouth is watering – we only got coffee.

"People are nasty when you hand out leaflets," she says. "And it was so cold. It felt like a total waste of time."

"It wasn't a waste, Amina," says Luke. His smile is so warm, I can't help but smile back. Amina, meanwhile, is looking at Noah.

"You go to our school, right?" she says.

Noah nods. He is kind of cute, I suppose, if you didn't know he was a wannabe vigilante. Actually, even then.

Noah swallows his coffee. "I'm in Year Ten. But not for long." He gestures at Luke. "We do maths together. Also art."

Luke hands Amina a fry and my chest tightens. Why didn't he like me? I'm almost grateful when Noah picks up one of Luke's leaflets and glances at it. "What's this about?" he asks.

"It's a talk my brother's helping organize. We're trying to raise awareness. A group of very powerful people are trying to exploit poor people…" Luke's glasses steam up with enthusiasm. I think about reaching over, removing them gently from his face, cleaning them, placing them gently back on his noble nose, perhaps with the lightest kiss…

My face is burning. It's hot in here.

"*Rothschild Zionist World Domination*," reads Noah. "*Who really controls the banks? Who was really behind 9/11?*" His face screws up in disgust. "What is this?"

"Why don't you come to the meeting? All welcome!"

Noah is shaking his head, very slowly. "Unbelievable," he says.

"I know," says Luke. "It is hard to believe. But it's true."

"Let's talk about something else," I interrupt quickly. "Did you see that show last night? You know, that one about teen mothers in America—"

Noah gets to his feet. He's still holding the leaflet. Then, slowly and deliberately, he tears it up.

"You," he says to Luke, "are a racist. You need to educate yourself."

Then he throws the tiny pieces up in the air and marches out.

They fall over us, like snowflakes.

"What," says Amina, "was *that* all about?"

Luke brushes the paper off his shoulder. "What is up with your friend?" he asks. I carefully push the pieces of paper into a pile, and then – because I can't think what else to do with them – put them into my pocket.

"I don't know what that was about," I say. "And he's not my friend. He's nothing to do with me."

Luke shakes his head. "Some people find the truth hard to take," he says.

"Oh, Noah's a total idiot," I say.

His smile is so kind. "I saw that your Mum had a hard time on Twitter," he says.

I'm not sure what to say, so I just nod.

"This could be a very powerful moment for her. If she would come out and speak up, on the right side – I could give you some material—"

They are holding hands. I've had enough.

I stand up. "I'm sorry," I say, "I'd better go."

"Are you feeling OK?" says Amina. "Shall I come with you?"

"No," I say. "I just need to go."

And then I turn and walk away.

When I get home I pull all the little bits of paper out of my pocket, and throw them into my bin.

One piece of paper misses the bin, so I pick it up. And I see the words written on it.

"*The international Jew*" it says.

I pull all the pieces out and I try and piece them together. I'm missing a few, but I can see enough.

The international Jew.

I have that horrible sick feeling again. But just to be sure I type it into Google. It says "a four-volume antisemitic work first published in the 1920s." It says "a particularly powerful tool for haters". It "portrays Jews as monolithic, malicious schemers, plotting to control the planet".

So the people Luke thinks exploit poor people, and secretly run the world … the secret, shadowy, group. it's Jews.

It's Mum. It's Lottie. It's even me.

And just like that, I fall out of love with Luke Braybourne.

CHAPTER TWENTY-NINE

LOTTIE

Evie's in the worst mood again. I'm not feeling great myself, because today we had art, and we were put in pairs and told to make a portrait of each other and I got put with Topaz. She's good at art, which made it all the nastier when she made my eyes look smaller and my nose look bigger, and Mel and Saffy both sniggered.

Anyway, Mum and Dad were out, so we made our own suppers – beans on toast for Evie, and vegetable soup for me. We eat in gloomy silence. They come in just as we're stacking the dishwasher.

"Girls," says Mum. "There's something we need to talk to you about."

That's when I notice how serious they look. Dad is holding Mum's hand. Immediately, I panic. Is one of them sick? Did Mum lose her job because of my tweet? Did something else bad happen, like the brick?

We follow them through to the living room and sit down. The window has already been mended, a red panic button installed, and we've been told to keep the curtains shut at all times, even though it's getting lighter in the evenings. These things are meant to make us feel safer, but they only make me feel more scared.

"Can you make this quick? I've got a history project to write," says Evie grumpily.

"Let Mum take her time," says Dad. "She's got something important to tell you."

We look at Mum, who is looking at her lap.

"It's not such a long story," she says, "and I should have told you a long time ago. It's just difficult, isn't it, to talk about sad things. Especially to children. You don't want them to realize how wicked people are."

"Bex, darling, why don't you start at the beginning?" says Dad. "Tell them about your father."

She nods. "My father – your grandfather – he was a difficult man. He was much older than my mother. I suppose he had depression, but no one ever used that word then. He was prone to bad moods."

Like Evie, I think.

"Periods when he wouldn't talk to us. He took to his bed. He couldn't talk. He became very protective of my mother and me – he wanted to know when we'd be in, what we were doing. I found it … oppressive. I knew he loved me, but I found him hard to live with. Impossible, in fact."

"It wasn't your fault," says Dad, and his voice is so gentle. "Anyone would have found it difficult."

"My father had every reason to be depressed and overprotective. He'd lost his family in the most terrible way."

She takes a deep breath. "He was born in

Hanover. His family had lived there for years. His father fought for the German army in the First World War. He was awarded an Iron Cross. They were Jewish – not particularly religious. Not then. They thought they were accepted. As German as anyone. But they were wrong."

I don't want to hear this. But Mum is telling us this story, that she never dared to tell us before, and it's important to listen. Even Evie has stopped scowling.

"He worked in his uncle's business. They imported and sold typewriters. Father was saving money, because his dream was to travel. Maybe to France or Italy – he loved art and music, he would have loved to have studied art." Her voice fades. She shakes her head. "I only know this because my mother told me. He would never talk to me about his life before he came to England. The war changed him in so many ways. He had no time for art and music after what had happened to him."

"It could have been a comfort to him," says Dad. "The art and music that he loved."

She shakes her head. "He felt guilty. He felt that he'd done something wrong. And that maybe if he hadn't loved art and music so much, then he might have, somehow, seen what was going to happen. He might have been able to escape – come to England earlier—"

"It wasn't easy to get a visa," says Dad. "People tried."

But my attention is on Mum. "That's why he always blamed himself," she says. "He constantly asked himself why he hadn't seized the chance to save the rest of his family when he might have been able to."

"Survivor guilt," says Dad.

"We know about that now. But we didn't then. I just thought he was overbearing and overprotective and miserable to live with. And I wanted to study drama and he wouldn't let me. It wasn't easy."

Evie finds her voice. "That must have been horrible for you," she says. "But why are you telling us now?"

CHAPTER THIRTY

EVIE

Mum reaches into her bag and pulls out a little cloth-covered wallet. I must have seen it in there a million times. I'd never looked in it.

She opens it and shows us. An old photograph of two teenage girls, one blonde, one dark. Their hair in plaits, they grin out at us from the past.

"This is the only photograph my father had of his two younger sisters. Charlotte and Eva."

"Like us!" I say.

"Their Hebrew names were Chaya Leah and Chava Rifka," she says. "I was called Rifka after my aunt."

"But your name is Bex," I say.

"Rifka is the Hebrew version of Rebecca. I was Rebecca at school. Bex came later on. I should have told you that you were named after them."

"Do we have Hebrew names too, then?"

"Most Jewish people have Hebrew names and English ones. Yours would be Chava – that's Eve – and Leah for Lottie.

Chava starts with a throaty sound – like the "ch" in loch that we learned about when we went on holiday to Scotland and it rained all week. I couldn't manage that sound. I can't even say my own secret name.

"What happened to them?" Lottie's voice is little more than a whisper.

"He never knew. Just that one word, *Auschwitz*. Where they were taken, along with fifty-seven members of his family. Aunts and uncles and cousins, grandparents, his parents... You can see why he found it so hard to live with the memories – imagining what might have happened to them.

"Do I need to explain what Auschwitz was? I always tried to protect you from the knowledge. You could learn about it at school, I thought. Millions of people – children, old people, teenagers like you – treated like vermin. Gassed and burned, or starved to death. Because bad people decided that they were to blame for everything. A system built to murder people on an industrial scale."

There are tears spilling out of her eyes and running down her cheeks. Lottie is crying too. But my eyes remain stubbornly dry. I feel nothing, except a very deep, icy anger. It's too big. It's too much.

"My father's whole family were gone. Religion was all he had left. He became very devout, very observant. It gave him … a way to keep on living. A rhythm to his days. And, I suppose, a way to feel he was defying Hitler.

"He never blamed God. He tried not to hate anyone. Eventually he met my mother and married her. She was younger, a rabbi's daughter. And after a few years, I was born.

"He couldn't let me be myself. He used religion as a way of keeping me safe. I hated it. I just wanted to be normal and free. As I got into my teenage years, we would argue. And then I felt guilty. When my mother got ill and died, it could have made us closer. It didn't."

"How old were you then?" Lottie's voice is thick with tears.

"I was seventeen. I went a little bit wild. I lived with my aunt for a while. Then, when I was eighteen, I went to Israel, volunteered on a kibbutz, a communal farm. We all worked together, cooked together, shared everything. It was amazing. I felt so free. I felt as though I'd come home.

"And then my father got sick and I came back to London. When he died, I had … well, I suppose you'd call it a breakdown. The guilt I felt for failing to make my dad happy. For being alive.

"I came through. I changed my name from Rifka – Rebecca – to Bex. I learned to smile and be positive. I put the past behind me, I started working in radio. And then I met my darling Alex." She grinned at my dad. "I had you girls. My life changed again."

You know those optical illusions, where you think you're looking at a man with a beard, but it's also the back view of a woman? That's how I feel. For the first time, I can see beyond my mum's smile and sparkle. I can see the whole person. The dark, sad, scared side of the Voice of Nice, our sparkly, funny mum.

"I made a decision. To bring you up away from the Jewish community, without a religion. I didn't want you to feel oppressed like I did. Maybe I did the wrong thing."

"Oh, Mum…" Lottie goes to hug her, which is clearly what I should have done.

"Why are you telling us this?" It comes out all wrong, bursting out of me, angry and accusing.

"I've been waiting for the right time," Mum says. "Too long, I know. But then Sarah told me her story, and then that brick through our window, the things people have been saying to me online… It made me feel like it was all happening again. All the hate. I started to feel like I was letting *them* down." She runs a finger over the photos. "I need to tell their story. Starting with you, but then, in a few weeks, on Metro. I've been given an opportunity."

She lifts her chin and her gaze is firm.

"I've been quiet for too long. It's time to speak."

CHAPTER THIRTY-ONE

LOTTIE

Dad asks if we want to talk more, and we both rush in with homework excuses, and go upstairs with our bags. Evie follows me into my bedroom.

"We're going to talk," she announces.

"We are?"

"I know you prefer your school friends, Swanky and Topaz … but this is important."

I shrug.

"Actually, I'm not really friendly with them any more."

"You're not?"

I hesitate. "I saw a nasty side to them. I didn't

want to be their friend any more. They weren't nice people."

"I could have told you that ages ago!" she says. But then, "I know how it feels when you find out that someone you liked is … not nice. Or worse."

"Amina?" I can't believe they would fall out.

"No. Someone else."

She's obviously not going to tell me, so I start telling her about Hannah, and Hannah's family and how I really want to be a super-Jew and keep kosher and celebrate the festivals and make Saturday into a day of rest. "I think it'll help with my stress levels. Just cutting off from normal life, shutting down my phone, you know…"

Evie snorts. "It sounds horrendous! No wonder Mum hated it."

"Mum hated the sadness in her home. But it doesn't have to be like that."

"You know, you're a bit like Mum," says Evie, thoughtfully.

"No I'm not." I can feel myself going pink. "You're much more like Mum than I am. Getting up on stage, making people laugh – I can totally see you as a radio presenter one day."

"I mean the way you always try and make things nice," says Evie.

"That's not true," I mutter.

"And by the way," she adds, "my comedy is *nothing* like Mum's Voice of Nice waffle."

She bats her eyelashes, "Hello everyone! Welcome back! Bex Harris here, helping you though the morning rush! Forget your troubles, tune out the commuter crush! We'll start off with some classic Elton John, and then I'll tell you what my twins got up to this weekend, bless their hearts."

I can't help giggling, although she's being mean. She's such a good mimic. "She'd never say 'bless their hearts'."

"She totally would. No, I just mean you insist you're OK, everything's fine, when you're not."

"I am!"

"No one's all right all the time. And no one should feel guilty just for existing. Not Mum and not you."

I don't know what she means.

"I'm not … I don't…"

"I can one-hundred per cent cope with you going to the posh expensive school. And I have totally got over you getting lots of attention because you were in hospital all that time. And I think it's horrible that you have asthma. So quit thinking you have to apologize for everything." She wrinkles her nose. "I never realized it but you're always trying to be the voice of nice."

"There's nothing wrong with nice," I say, and then I realize that I sound just like Mum.

"You can be religious if you want," says Evie, generously. "But stop thinking you have to be a hundred per cent good. No one is. It's impossible. Even those girls, Mum's aunts, they would have grown up to be real people. They should have grown up. It's just so unfair that they didn't."

Unfair. I mean there's no word, is there, to say just how wrong it was, what happened to our grandfather's family. There's no word big or strong enough. Words like "unfair" and "sad" and

210

"terrible" are like tiny pebbles, standing in for huge volcanoes.

Or maybe there are bigger, better words and I just haven't learned them yet.

"It is frightening," I say. "Because if it could happen to them, it could happen to us."

"Well, I refuse to be frightened. OK, some monster threw a brick through our window. But we're not going to be marched off to an extermination camp. This is Britain! It's the Twenty-first century. I don't care what Noah says. Things like that just don't happen any more."

"They do, in some places," I point out, wondering what Noah's been saying to her. "In Syria. In China. In Africa."

"OK, OK. But not in Britain."

There's a silence. *Yes, in Britain*, I think. Maybe not concentration camps, but it's there, the threat of terrorism. I think of the security guard outside the synagogue.

But I don't say any of this to Evie, because I can see that her anger and her courage and her refusal to be scared is another version of what

Mum and I do when we make nice. Maybe Evie's jokes and tantrums come from the same place as my fear and anxiety.

We thought we didn't know Mum's story. We didn't know the facts. But, in some mysterious way, we've known it all our lives.

CHAPTER THIRTY-TWO

LOTTIE

I dither about whether I should tell Mum and Dad that I'm going to Hannah's sister's batmitzvah. In the end I do. Partly because I'm fed up with lying, and partly because after what Mum told us, it feels wrong somehow.

It's fine. Dad offers to give me a lift and Mum asks which synagogue it is, and when I tell her she says it's the one she used to go to when she was growing up. "You'll have to sit in a ladies' gallery and watch the men run the service," she says. "I used to get so bored."

Then I tell her that actually I've been before,

and at Purim the women had their own service, and she is amazed.

All the way I'm anxious about being late. Hannah told me not to worry, that no one would be there dead on, but I hate being late for anything.

But I'm also excited. I wonder what a batmitzvah will be like. I wonder whether I could have one some day. Girls at school have told me about theirs – about the parties mostly – but for me it wouldn't be about that. It would be about feeling part of something. Marking out my intention to identify as a Jewish person for the rest of my life.

Dad glances over at me. "You're excited, aren't you?" he says. "You really like all this?"

"Yes," I say, knowing he'll understand. "It feels right, you know. It feels like I belong. And it feels … especially after Mum told us about Grandpa, sort of important."

He's smiling.

"That's good," he says. "I always wanted you to know what it meant to be Jewish. I knew I had two Jewish daughters, and I wanted them to know what that meant."

"Why did it matter to you?"

He rumples his hair, screws up his face. Normally that would mean he's about to tell a joke, but this time he's dead serious.

"You never met my parents, Lottie. I ought to be sad about that, but actually, I don't think you ever would have met."

"Why not?"

"My parents were well off. Sent me to boarding school. They were what I'd call, old-fashioned antisemites. Thought Jewish people were, you know, *not quite like us*. Not quite trustworthy. 'Not really our sort of people'."

He mimics Granny's long-dead posh voice.

"Were they racist about other people as well?"

"They didn't know anyone from other backgrounds. This wasn't multicultural London, this was very, very white Hampshire. And when I met your mum... Well, she wasn't what they were expecting."

"Oh, Dad, that's awful."

"We just went off and got married with our friends there. Auntie Vera – she's as tough as old boots, and she supported us. My parents hardly saw us again. I think they saw you girls once. It was hard to feel sad when they died. It was more of a relief.

"I knew it was complicated for your mum and I understood why. But I wanted you to know your heritage." He smiles, eyes on the road. "I admit, I never expected one of you to become properly religious."

"I'm just … exploring at the moment," I say. "I'm looking for *my* way of being Jewish."

"You know," he says, "what with your mum's show, and me and my sitcom and Evie wanting to do stand up, maybe we don't spend enough time just talking to each other."

I want to tell him how nice it was having Friday night dinner at Hannah's house, how much I'd like our family to do it. But I'm not quite ready to admit I'd been lying as much as I have been.

He stops the car, and points to a couple in

front of us, walking along the platform. They're both wearing hats.

"Here we are," he says. "Follow those two. It's just around the corner."

"How do you know that's where they're going?"

"Men and women cover their heads in the synagogue. I know a lot!"

I put my phone in the glove compartment. You can't use electrical equipment on the Sabbath, and it's actually a nice relief to switch it off, to stem the flow of anxiety-inducing posts and comments and chats. It's like stepping out of the city into a beautiful, green forest. "You know where to pick me up?"

"Hannah's house at ten p.m.," he says. "Have a great time, lovely Lottie. Enjoy yourself."

CHAPTER THIRTY-THREE

EVIE

I'm on the Tube heading for north London. I'm going to meet Noah and his Avengers. There's something that they can do for me.

I didn't think he'd agree, but I told him I'd realized he was right about Luke. That there was so much I had been ignoring and denying even to myself. In the end, I think he said yes just to shut me up.

He meets me at the station and we walk together to his friend's house. "Hang on," I say. "It's Saturday morning. You're not going to synagogue?"

"Nope," he says. "I don't go without my dad. It's something we do together."

"What's happening about your dad? Is he coming to England?"

"Not England, no." He's smiling. "Dad won't leave France for England but he says he will live in Israel – that is, if I can persuade Mum."

"Israel! But it's a war zone, isn't it? And they're really mean to the Palestinian people."

He sighs. "Where do you get your information from?"

"Well, you know … everyone knows that."

"*Everyone knows that*," he mimics me. "Look, there's a lot to say about Israel and Palestine and we could be here all day if I tried to explain all the background. But you should try and read about it. It's more complicated than you think." He glances at me. "I could recommend you some books, if you'd like?"

I want to tell him that history isn't my subject – but I know what he'll say. That it should be. That I can't skitter around on the surface of an argument without knowing the facts.

"Wouldn't you have to serve in the army if you go and live there?" I ask.

"I'd be proud to defend the Jewish homeland," he says.

There's nothing I can think of to answer that.

"Here we are," he says.

His friend lives on a council estate, in a little house with no front garden. He's scrawny and scruffy, with huge glasses and big eyes. He's a head shorter than Noah, and a head taller than me. "This is Benny," says Noah. "Benny, this is Evie. The one who gate-crashed our last mission."

"Hi, Evie." His smile is warm and friendly. "Come and meet Leo. Zak's not here, he's got a batty."

Avenger HQ is Benny's bedroom, which is just about big enough for a single bed, a desk and a computer with three screens. Leo is lounging on the bed, but sits up when we come in. He's tall and blond and nothing like as friendly as Benny.

"What's she doing here again?" he demands.

"We can't afford security breaches, man."

Noah shrugs. "She's very persistent. And she's a victim of antisemitism, herself."

Benny and Leo look at me. "Someone threw a brick through our window," I tell them.

"Must have been very scary," says Benny.

"It really was," I say. "I'm worried it was that guy, you know, whose house you threw paint at. What if he followed me home to south London?"

"It doesn't sound very likely," says Benny. "Did you stop on the way home?"

"Noah and I went to a café…" I say.

Leo snorts. "Then that doesn't make any sense. You think he followed you to a café, waited outside, then followed you all the way back to south London?"

I nod. He's right. But I don't feel any better.

"He's exactly the sort of person who would send tweets like that," says Benny. "But I doubt it was him that threw the brick. He's just a keyboard warrior."

I look around his room, at the laptops and

computers. "Can you find the people who have been saying stuff to my mum?" I ask suddenly.

Benny shrugs. "Yeah. Of course I can."

I sink on to the bed. "How about we find one of them and I go and see them."

They all stare at me.

"Why?" says Noah, at last. "This isn't some sort of reality show, Evie. You don't get to find a troll and tell him how bad he made you feel and make the world better."

I shake my head. "I know," I say. "And I don't want to paint graffiti on their door either or let down their tyres or scratch their paintwork. I just want to see one of them."

Benny's eyes are sympathetic. "You think it'll help, to see what hate looks like?"

"I think so. I'm making whoever did this into a monster in my mind, and I can't sleep at night, and … just seeing them will help. I think."

"Then I think I've got the man for you. Just identified him."

Benny turns to his computer.

"Benny's a computer whizzkid," says Noah.

"He hacks into chatrooms, he monitors haters, he knows how to track down actual people from their IP addresses."

Benny turns round. "There you go. King Troll. Keith Barton. He's very active. He's the one who told your mum to go put her head in a gas oven. Finish what Hitler started…"

"Ugh. Why do people put so much energy into being so nasty, when they could be nice?" I say.

Noah laughs. "Isn't that your mum's line? The Voice of Nice. I can imagine her wanting to meet a troll to talk to them, not throw paint."

He says it like it's a compliment. And I don't feel embarrassed to be compared to Mum, like I once would. I feel proud. "Keith Barton lives about half a mile from here," says Benny. "Are we up for this?"

And just like that, we go.

As we walk there, I'm feeling more and more nervous. I glance over at Noah. He looks totally calm.

If I can do this, I think, *I can do anything*.

"This is the street," says Noah, glancing around. We're standing on a completely ordinary London street. Who would think that inside one of these houses there's someone sitting who thinks it's fine to issue threats against someone he's never met?

"Here," says Benny. "Number thirty-seven."

Numbers thirty-five and thirty-nine, either side of Keith Troll's house, are neat and well painted. The gardens are full of tulips and daffodils. Number thirty-five has some bright and cheery gnomes.

Number thirty-seven isn't like that. It's painted white, but it's grey with grime, and the paint is peeling. The front garden is concreted over and is full of dustbins and rubbish. A sopping wet mattress. A rusting bike. I muster every tiny bit of courage that I have in my body.

"You'll call the police if he … if anything…" I can't even finish the sentence.

"We're right here," says Benny. "You are not on your own. Do you want us to come with you to the door?"

"No, it's OK," I say firmly. "Go and hide behind a tree or something."

I take a deep breath. Here I go. Evie Harris, the new Voice of Nice. Trying to do things a different way.

I march up to the front door and, hand shaking, ring the bell.

Nothing. No answer. I'm just about to heave a sigh of relief and scuttle down the path, when I hear a shuffling noise inside, and the door creaks open.

The man looking at me is very small and very bald. He's wearing pyjamas and a dressing gown. He peers through thick glasses. And his voice is high, like a young boy's, although he must be at least forty.

"What do you want?"

"Are you Keith Barton?"

"Who wants to know?"

"I'm Evie," I say, finding my courage. "I think you're known as King Troll on Twitter?"

"So what if I am? There are lots of King Trolls on Twitter."

He's right about that.

"You wrote horrible things about my mum," I say. "You said you should put her head in a gas oven."

"Wait." He stares at me. "*Your mum* is Bex Harris?"

"Yes," I say.

"Well." He gathers himself. "She can't take a bit of banter? Those tweets, they were just jokes."

That makes me angry. I know comedy, and those tweets aren't it. "Saying someone should die isn't a joke! Jokes are funny, for one."

"It is a joke," he says, "because I say it is. And I find it funny, so what's your problem?" He laughs, and I take a step back.

"You're sick," I say. "And pathetic. And you'd never make it as a stand-up. And I should tell the police where you live."

"Go ahead. I'd like to point out that you are on my property here," he says. "Trespassing."

"I just – I wanted you to know that there are real people getting hurt," I say, but I know there's no point.

"Keith! Keith!" It's an old woman's voice, and it's coming from inside the house.

"Coming," he yells back.

"Is that your mum?" I ask. His expression flickers.

"What would she think of you? If she could see the things you write? Do you think she'd find them funny?

Keith's mouth turns down at the side, like a little kid who's been found out stealing ginger nuts from the cookie jar.

"Shall I tell her? Shall I keep coming round till I speak to her?"

That hits home. Keith flushes.

"Go away! Go away! Stop harassing me!"

"Better stop the trolling then," I say. "I'll be watching."

As I walk back down the path, I feel as tall as Lottie.

"You were talking for ages," says Benny. "Go on. What happened?"

So I explain as we walk up the road and they all look impressed, even Noah. I feel good.

Strong and brave and powerful.

Leo's phone pings, and he looks at his messages. And all the colour drains from his face.

"It's Zak," he says. "He's at the shul. It's under attack."

CHAPTER THIRTY-FOUR

LOTTIE

"Are you here for the batmitzvah?" a lady asks me as I approach the synagogue gate. There are two others with her, alongside the security guard. "Yes – I'm a friend of Hannah's," I explain.

She smiles. "You're here nice and early." She points me towards a side door. "In that way, and then up the stairs."

Am I *too* early, I wonder, as I climb the stairs. There don't seem to be any other people around. I'm nervous, and now I'm wondering if I'm wearing the right thing. I'm wearing my tartan skirt and navy jumper. Mum was very insistent that I had to have long sleeves and a skirt at least on the knee. "Unless things have changed a lot, that's what they'll expect," she said. She had smiled at me and pushed back a strand of my hair. "It feels so strange that you're going back there."

There's a small cloakroom at the top of the stairs. I hang up my coat and walk through the door at the far side of the room, which takes me to another empty room. There's a door at the far end, so I walk through, wondering if I'm destined to go on and on, walking through empty rooms until I get back to the stairs and out again.

But behind the next door is something quite different. Space and light and music. It takes a moment to get my bearings.

I'm up in a gallery which stretches around three walls of the room. There are a few other women dotted around in rows of seats, and in the front row a line of hats with Hannah and Dalya's curly heads at the end. Down below are rows of seats, some of them occupied by men, also grouped around three sides of the room. On the other wall there's a low stage, and at the back, a set of velvet curtains, flanked by pillars.

In the very middle of the room is a raised platform, with a some benches, and a big tabletop, covered with a dark blue velvet cloth with gold embroidery which I think is lettering – it's hard to tell from here. At the table stands a man, and he is singing.

He's not performing – he has his back to most of the people. There are no musical instruments, no choir.

The tunes are both strange and familiar, sad tunes in a minor key. Sometimes the people listening join in, sometimes he just sings by himself.

I wish more than anything that I understood the Hebrew words.

"Hey! Lottie!" Hannah comes over. "Thanks for coming!"

She's wearing trousers, I realize, black ones, under a dark purple tunic. "Mum let me wear them," she whispers, as she hands me two books, a small green one and a large, heavy blue one. "You're not really meant to, but she said that she'd rather I was happy than feeling all wrong." She grins. "Anyway, no one has said anything."

That's possibly because no one is here yet, I think, looking at the empty seats for women. The only row that is full is the front one, and that's for Hannah's family. She finds me a seat just behind her. "We're here", she says opening the smaller book and showing me the place, "and when it comes to swapping to the other book I'll tell you."

"Why is no one here?"

"People come later," she says. "They only need ten men to start." She rolls her eyes. "Women don't count, of course."

The room begins to fill up, with men bustling around downstairs and women coming past me to kiss Hannah's mum and congratulate her. Dalya's sitting next to her, swinging her legs, clutching a ring binder that I guess contains her speech. She looks nervous, but excited too, waving to her friends on the opposite side of the gallery. There's a buzz of whispered chat – and sometimes the man leading the service stops and bangs his hand on the velvet surface in front of him to make people quieten down.

Then there's a lull and everyone stands up and the curtains at the front are opened to reveal a cabinet of silver and blue objects.

I watch as two men take ancient-looking scrolls out of the cabinet, and carry them carefully to the central desk. One is carefully unwrapped – first the silver adornments, then the velvet cover – and unrolled, and Hannah finds my place in the second book, which turns out to be the first five books of the Bible.

There are quite a few men on the platform now, all gathered around the scroll. I watch as Hannah's dad joins them, and says a prayer, and then takes the silver pointer that they use to pick out the words on the scroll, and starts to sing – or chant – what's written there.

"Men, men, men," Hannah mutters and I realize then that there aren't any women downstairs, except one little girl on her dad's knee.

I have never thought much about God. But if people survived years of persecution and violence and this prayer, this ritual, this singing, this lifting of scrolls, this standing up and sitting down – if all of this was at the heart of what bound them together, then it's worth learning about. It's worth being part of.

There are more prayers, more singing. And then it's Dalya's moment.

She's downstairs, all ready, her blue dress standing out among the dark suits as she waits at her dad's side. She's nervous, I can tell, but her voice is steady as she starts to speak.

"We have heard about the work that the Israelites put into building a house for God, the holy temple—"

Then she stops. Because somewhere close at hand – inside? Outside? – we hear a woman scream.

CHAPTER THIRTY-FIVE

EVIE

"Under attack?" I echo. The boys are all staring at their phones, looking on Twitter.

"It doesn't say much," says Noah. "It must have just happened…"

"We should go there?" says Benny.

"But what can we do?" asks Leo, and Benny shrugs.

And then it strikes me.

"Lottie – she went to a batmitzvah today."

Noah stares at me. "Probably a different one. Don't worry…"

I try her phone but it goes to voicemail. I leave

a message "Lottie? Are you OK? Call me."

"It's not far from here," says Benny. "Come on."

We start to run. "Maybe there's something we can do to help," pants Benny. "I hope your sister isn't there…"

We run past shops and houses, cross roads, turn corners. Their legs are longer than mine, but I keep up with them.

"We can cut through here," says Noah, turning into a smelly alleyway, full of bins and rubbish, with cobbles underfoot.

I hear sirens wailing in the distance. *What if we get there before the police?* I think, and I don't know if the reason my heart is pounding so much is because I'm scared or because I'm running so fast.

And then my phone rings – Lottie, must be – and I fumble for it, but it drops out of my hand and skids into the gutter.

"You go ahead," I gasp. I scoop up my phone. The screen is smashed so badly that I can't see who called me.

I stab at it. "Lottie?" I say, "Lottie?" But there's no answer.

CHAPTER THIRTY-SIX

LOTTIE

Everyone seems to know what to do. Hannah grabs my hand, and we follow her mum and the rest of her family, hurrying down the stairs, into the main synagogue space and then through another door and down some more stairs into a windowless basement. Maybe a hundred people, all squashed in together, a bare, empty space with just a few chairs. The most elderly people are being helped to sit down.

The rest of us are standing or sitting on the floor. There's a buzz of whispered conversations, parents reassuring their children, an old lady asking, "What happened? Why are we here?" and her daughter trying to reassure her: "Don't worry, Mum, nothing to be scared of. We'll be out very soon. It's just a drill."

"Is it?" I whisper to Hannah, and she shakes her head.

"In the middle of Dalya's batty? No way."

"Here, in the corner," says her mum and we squeeze on to a blanket that someone's put on the dusty concrete floor. "Are you all right, Lottie? I hope this is a false alarm."

Dalya's still clutching her ring binder file. Her eyes are huge and dark, and she's very still. Her mum is rubbing her back, but Dalya pulls away. When another lady – an aunt, perhaps – comes over and tries to talk to her, Dalya puts her hands over her face. She's trying to hide her tears, but they drip down her chin.

The doors bang behind us. A man locks the door and pulls a security grille closed over it.

I'm trying not to panic. A baby is crying. A little girl is shouting, "I don't like it! I don't like it!" I don't like it either.

Hannah lets go of my hand, as though she's surprised she's still holding it, and gives me a good attempt at a smile.

She opens her mouth to speak but just then the rabbi standing on the stairs blows a whistle, and everyone stops talking. The baby's still wailing, and the sound is almost unbearable.

"I'm so sorry to have to disturb everyone and interrupt Dalya's speech," he says. "We have a credible threat against our shul. The police have been called, and they are on their way. We have been asked to stay here, quiet and safe, until the threat is over. We don't know how long that will be, and I know it is not very comfortable in here, but it is necessary. Please God we will all come out safe and well."

Voices rise in questions. *Where's Ruth? Where's Andy? Where's Marek?*

"They were on security duty," Hannah whispers in my ear. "Ruth and Andy. Ruth taught me at Hebrew classes when I was younger. Andy runs my brother's football team. Marek is the shul's security guard. I hope they're all OK."

A credible threat. *A terrorist*, I think, it must be.

Girls my age, going to a pop concert in Manchester, so excited. People enjoying a night out in London. Commuters going to work on a busy London Tube. People praying in a synagogue in Pittsburgh. And in a mosque in New Zealand. And more and more and more. My mouth is dry, my heart thundering hard. Am I going to be one of them? Am I going to die?

I imagine Mum and Dad and Evie hearing the news and how scared they'll be, and it's that thought – their faces – that brings tears to my eyes.

Hannah squeezes my hand. "It'll be OK," she says, but even her calm voice is a bit shaky.

Hannah's dad is in a corner with some other men, and I can see that they are praying, silently, rocking backwards and forwards, wrapped in their black and white prayer shawls. One brother is with us, the other is praying too.

"Do you want a tissue?" I whisper to Dalya, and when she nods I pass her the clean one I have in my pocket. She scrubs at her eyes and blows her nose, and whispers, "Thanks, Lottie."

Can I read your speech?" I ask, trying to cheer her up. "I was enjoying it. You were doing amazingly."

She nods, eyes shiny, and passes me the papers clutched in her hand. I sit and read it. It's good. I like the way she talks about God taking different forms – a cloud, a fire – and how those forms can protect us, or warm us, or guide us. And how God is not distant from us, but all around us, not a person but a presence, not one thing, or any gender but multiple, indefinable, infinite and boundless.

It's not at all what I thought the Jewish idea of God was, which was basically some mean old man with a beard. But then no one Jewish ever explained Judaism to me before.

"It's so good," I say, handing it back to her, and she mouths, "Thank you," to me.

"I wish we knew what was happening," says her mother, biting her lip. "Oh, Lottie. Your first Shabbat service."

"It's OK," I say. "I'm OK."

But I'm not. It's hot in here, and although people keep reassuring each other that there's plenty of ventilation, the air already feels stale. My throat is closing up, and my breath is getting harder to catch. I can hear myself starting to wheeze.

I feel in my pocket for my inhaler. But it isn't there.

CHAPTER THIRTY-SEVEN

EVIE

I fumble with my phone, trying to get it to turn on. I give up.

I shove it in my pocket and turn to head after the boys. They're only a few metres ahead of me.

And then I see the man.

He's right at the top of the alleyway, crouched behind a bin, dressed all in black. He's hiding. Just as you might if you didn't want to be caught by the police. If you'd just attacked a synagogue. If you were a terrorist.

I see that in his hand there's a huge knife, glinting bright in a shaft of sunlight.

I let out a tiny whimpering noise, the sound of fear. He looks around.

The boys are nearly level with him.

"Stop!" I yell, and I hurtle down the alley, as fast as I can. The boys scatter, their faces startled. I grab a huge wheelie bin and aim it at the man, pushing it at him, with as much force as I can muster. Noah and Leo run on, past the bin, but Benny stumbles and falls – too near to him, too near to that terrible blade.

The bin ricochets back towards me, slamming into me, knocking me back against the wall.

The man stands over Benny, and raises his knife.

"No!" I yell, and push the bin back towards them again.

Then I close my eyes, and wait to die.

CHAPTER THIRTY-EIGHT

LOTTIE

Hannah leans towards me. "Lottie? Are you OK?"

I can only shake my head.

"Do you have your inhaler?"

Again, I shake my head.

Hannah's mum calls out. "Has anyone got an inhaler? This girl's having an asthma attack."

One of the men praying in the corner immediately puts down his book and pushes through the crowd towards us. "I'm a doctor," he says. Someone else offers an inhaler.

I take it and breathe in… One, two, three… It's better. But I can't get to ten.

"A little better?" says the doctor. I nod.

"OK, let's try and clear the space around her..."

There's a little more air, a little more relief. I try the inhaler again. This time I manage to count to eight.

"Just breathe," says Hannah's mum. "Come on Lottie. Just breathe."

And suddenly, Evie comes into my mind. It's as though she's there next to me. And she's saying, "Come on, Lottie, you can do this. You can get through this." So I concentrate, and steady myself.

"That's good," says the doctor. "Well done. That's good."

"We're safe, we're going to get out of here," says Hannah's mum. "It's scary, but we will be all right. We will come through this. And tomorrow I want to see you dancing at Dalya's party."

It all helps. My breathing steadies. I take another puff of the inhaler. And this time it seems to work, and my chest starts working with me, and my breathing is quieter and easier and I don't feel so scared any more.

"That's more like it," says the doctor.

"Well done," says Hannah's mum, taking my hand. "Brave girl."

More time goes by. The air in the room is stale and smelly. People stop talking, they sit, leaning on each other, rocking babies, soothing children, praying softly.

And then, at last, there is a knock on the door. A shout of "Police". The security grille is pushed back, the door is opened, and we are led out, blinking into the grey, overcast daylight.

CHAPTER THIRTY-NINE

EVIE

A loud noise and blood and the smell of ancient takeaways. And pain and darkness and that silver knife, flashing though the air, and…

"Evie?"

How do you know my name? I want to ask, but my brain isn't in synch with my voice, and when I open my mouth – which is quite an effort – I just manage a weird, groaning sound. Everything hurts, from the top of my head to my fingers and toes.

"We're getting you to hospital." I must look really out of it, because the voice repeats more slowly. "We're getting you to hos-pit-al. You're in an am-bu-lance."

"Good," I croak and then I am very sick, mostly into a grey bowl. After that I just close my eyes and try not to think about the man … the knife … the man…

I wake up again when they carry me out of the ambulance… *I'm on a stretcher … I must be really ill* … and then there is noise and people and lights and someone saying my name, and then a sharp, burning pain in my arm and the pain fades away and then so does everything else.

When I wake up – with a huge headache – Lottie is at my side.

I freeze, panic washing over me.

"It's OK," she says. "They got him. He can't hurt you. He can't hurt any of us."

"Lottie? I thought … I was so scared…"

"So was I," she says. She's pale. She takes my hand in mine and we grip tight.

Normally I'd make a joke, to cheer us both up, but I don't have anything in me that's funny right now.

"I'll tell the nurse that you're awake," she says, "and Mum and Dad should be here any minute … stuck in traffic, would you believe, they're frantic…"

"No – first – tell me what happened. There was a man, a knife…" I think back. "And Noah! Is he OK? And Benny!"

"They're getting treatment I think, for cuts and scratches, but you saved them. They're all safe. Evie, you were amazing."

"I was?" It's like looking at a blurry picture and then everything coming back into focus. "There was a bin…"

"All I know is that when we came out of the synagogue Noah was there waiting. And he said that you'd saved his life, and saved his friends, and we had to come to the hospital right away."

Now I remember. The bin, crashing into me. The pain in my head. And the man, standing over me, knife in hand, shouting about death and Jews…

"Did he stab me?" I have dressings on my face, I can feel them.

"No, the police caught him. You've had X-rays to check. You got bruises and scratches and they've bandaged them up but that's all. You're OK."

She breathes in, a long breath and adds, "You'll think I'm mad. But I could feel you, I knew you were in trouble."

"I knew you were in the synagogue," I say. "Even though you didn't say which one, I knew."

We sit there in silence for a moment, holding hands.

"The man," I say. "Why?"

"I don't know. He wanted to kill Jews. Does it matter who he is and what he thought he was doing?"

Yes, I think, and then no. When haters hate that much, their reasons don't matter. They are so scared of the lies they believe about Jews, that they want to kill innocent people.

That is what we are scared of.

And that includes me.

CHAPTER FORTY

LOTTIE

I sit with Evie, and watch her sleep. The nurses warned me that she'd be exhausted and she was pumped full of pain killers, and so we just sit quietly, and when she wakes up I tell her everything is all right, and then she goes to sleep again.

Hannah's mum sits with me some of the time, and then when Mum and Dad arrive she explains everything she can about what happened, and tells them that I was very brave while we were all in the basement. It's too much all of a sudden, and I can't deal with it. I start trembling and Mum says, "Lottie, darling, you've gone very pale," and Dad fishes half a KitKat out of his pocket and insists I eat it, which makes me feel slightly better.

Then Mum asks when I last ate, and I realize it's breakfast time.

So Dad says he'll stay with Evie and talk to the doctor and the police, while Mum takes me down to the hospital cafeteria to get some food and Hannah's mum goes home. Dad promises that he'll call Mum right away when Evie wakes up.

At the cafeteria I can't decide what I want to eat, so Mum sits me down at a table and comes back with a trayful of food. A baguette with tuna and cucumber. A croissant. Some tomato soup. Another KitKat. Some fruit salad. A bottle of orange juice. A cup of tea.

"So much food!" I say.

"I didn't know what you'd want, and I thought … there must be something here…"

I see then, how much pain it causes when I nibble at the edges of the meals she makes. How much love is poured into those meals, and how unable I was to accept that love, because I wanted something different from her.

What did I want?

Maybe I have to take the first step.

So I tear off the end of the croissant, and spread some jam on it, and eat. It is sweet and comforting, and with the hot tea makes me feel much better. In between bites I tell her everything. About Saffy and Hannah, about being Jewish and how I feel about it, about the batmitzvah, and what it was like being down in the basement.

"It was horrible, it was so scary, but the people were kind and nice and … I don't want to be so scared that I never go again. I think I need to go again."

She listens. She nods sympathetically, she holds my hand, she focuses all her attention on me, just me, and once I've finished – and moved on to the baguette, because I am starving – she says, "But why did you keep so much secret from us, darling Lottie?"

"Because … I didn't think you'd be happy," I tell her.

She shakes her head. "I'm sorry. I wanted you

to grow up free of my past – of fear and sadness and all the horrors – but all I did was pass it on in a different way. I should have had more faith in your ability to cope."

I don't know what to say, but then I see Noah and his Mum coming towards us.

"Bex!"

"Sarah!"

Noah's arm is in plaster, and he looks pale and tired, like Evie, and spaced out like her too. They sit down next to us. I push the orange juice and KitKat and fruit salad towards him.

"What happened to Evie?" he blurts out. "Is she all right?"

"Evie's OK," I reassure him. "She's just got cuts and bruises, and they're going to do some X-rays. But she'll be all right."

"She just disappeared under that bin – I thought he'd kill both of them, her and Benny—"

"She's OK," I repeat. "She's really OK."

He looks relieved. He says, "Tell her she was right. We're stopping all the stuff we were doing. There's no point making things worse."

"What stuff?" I ask, but he shakes his head. "She'll understand."

Sarah's telling Mum that this has made up their mind. London isn't safe, nor is Paris. They'll be moving to Israel in the summer. "We'll start again from scratch. It's the only place we can feel safe."

I understand; but I'm also sad that they feel that way. That the thing that they were scared of came and found them in London. Can they really ever feel safe? Can I?

Maybe they can, in a country where Jews are in charge. But it's a tiny country, surrounded by enemies, with loads of problems of its own, and I know Noah will have to go into the army one day.

"Maybe we can visit you some time?" I say, and Noah grins and says, "I think that's a given."

We get up to go back to Evie and Sarah says, "She saved Noah's life. We can never thank her enough. What a girl."

"She's incredibly brave," I say. And I'm so proud of my twin, I can't stop grinning.

CHAPTER FORTY-ONE

EVIE

I am home and watching TV with a soft fluffy blanket over me, and feather pillows propping me up, and Mum popping in every two minutes to top up my hot chocolate and offer to make me toast.

Normally I'd be really irritated by now – there's only so much mothering I can take – but I feel so achy and bruised, jumpy and jittery that I don't really mind. I jolt whenever I hear a loud noise, sure there's a man behind me. Or that a brick will come through the window. It's trauma, says Mum.

It's drained all the funny out of me. I can't imagine doing stand-up now. I'm preparing myself for a nice quiet future, working in a hushed library perhaps. Or I could be a shepherdess. Or maybe one of those scientists in the Antarctic.

Noah's messaged me a few times. *Thank you for saving my life*, he said. I know I have to reply, but I just can't pull the words together in my head.

Benny messaged me too, saying thank you as well and telling me he was giving up troll hunting. He asked what sort of comedy I like, and he's been sending me little clips from YouTube of stuff he likes, which is pretty similar to my taste. He says that when I feel better he'd like to take me to a comedy club he knows to say thank you. It's a nice idea, but I feel exhausted just thinking about it.

Mum pops in again – "Look who's here, Evie! It's Amina!"

I am not ready to see anyone. I have stitches on my chin, and bruises puffing out the side of my face. I can't imagine I look great.

"Oh, Evie!" Amina's eyes are huge as she takes in how I look.

"She's had a nasty fall," says Mum. "I'll get some hot chocolate."

Officially, I am off school because I supposedly fell off my bike. This is because Mum and Dad (and the police) think that extremists like the man they've arrested might target us if they knew my name. But unofficially Lottie texted Amina and told her everything. "Because she is your best friend, and this is too big a secret to hide from her," she insisted. I didn't argue. I'm done with keeping secrets from my friend.

"I'm so sorry, Evie," Amina whispers. "This must have been terrifying."

"I don't want to talk about it," I say. And I really don't.

Amina leans forward. "I'm here to apologize. Your friend Noah was totally on it about Luke."

"Luke?" I can barely remember who he is.

"Those leaflets. When I got home, I checked them out online. And I showed them to my Mum. And, well basically, they were awful. Full of racist crap about Jewish people. I never realized it was that bad. I feel so ashamed that I was handing out racist stuff. Obviously I've split up with Luke—"

"You what?"

"And then you nearly died in some awful terrorist attack and—"

She's sobbing and that sets me off, and Mum has to bring in some tissues till we reach the hiccoughing stage and calm down again.

"I feel like I was a bad friend to you!" says Amina. "I didn't know Luke was into conspiracy theories. And I hate that people think that all Muslims are terrorists…"

"Only really stupid, ignorant people think that," I say. "And when it comes to Luke, I was stupid too. I thought he was so smart. To be honest, I kind of had a teeny, tiny crush on him."

She gives me a watery smile. "That makes me feel better for falling for him. Mum couldn't see why I liked him at all."

"Your Mum is wonderful, Amina," says Mum. "She got in touch a few weeks ago, when there was such a big reaction to my radio show, and she wants me to go along to a meeting of a group she goes to – for Jewish and Muslim women—"

"They are doing a vigil for peace at the synagogue tomorrow," says Amina, "We could all go…" But then she looks at me and says "Too soon?"

I force a smile. "Yup. Way too soon."

"Maybe Lottie and I could go with her," says Mum. "I think she needs to go back."

"I was thinking…" says Amina. "About what we could do, Evie. To make sure people like Luke don't keep spreading that rubbish."

"What can we do?" I say helplessly. "He's got all these people hanging off his every word."

"Nah, he just spouts the crap his brother tells him. We can fight back with *facts*."

"Like what?"

"Like, there are 1.8 billion Muslims in the world, and really a very small proportion of them support extremists. And there are only 14.7 million Jews in the world, which is actually a really tiny number. People don't know this kind of thing!"

Mum is blinking with amazement at Amina's statistical knowledge. I could have told her that my friend eats facts for breakfast.

"That's a great idea," Mum says.

"And who's going to listen to us? How are we sharing all these facts?" I say.

"TikTok," says Amina. "We can dance. We can rap. We can do a bit of stand-up – and we can explain really difficult bits of history and politics to people."

"Oh!" I feel a jolt of energy going through my brain. A vision of Amina and me, schooling the world. It could be completely amazing.

It could also bring hate and threats and bricks flying through our windows.

"I'll think about it," I say.

CHAPTER FORTY-TWO

LOTTIE

Evie's bruises fade and her scars heal, and she goes back to school and everything's meant to be normal again. But it isn't. She's not the same.

She's stopped cracking jokes. She shrugs when I ask her about her comedy workshop and her stand-up routines. She seems tired all the time. She's just picking at her food.

No one knows what to do. Even Amina has stopped trying to get her to do some TikTok project that she's thought up.

One day, Dad gets an email about a talk at the Jewish Museum and decides we should all go.

"It's by a wonderful woman called Mala Tribich, a Holocaust survivor, who was just about the girls' age during the war. We should hear her story."

"I don't know," Mum says uneasily. "The girls have been through so much."

"It might help," says Dad. "It might make them feel stronger to hear her story."

So we go, and the room is packed to hear Mala Tribich speak.

She has shining blonde hair, and a beautiful face. The man introducing her says she is nearly ninety, but it is quite unbelievable. She looks much younger. When she speaks, her voice is also younger than her age. It's easy to imagine her as a girl telling us her story.

CHAPTER FORTY-THREE

MALA'S TESTIMONY

I came from the Polish town, Piotrkow-Tribulnalski, a very old, pretty town with classical architecture, a beautiful park and squares. I was brought up in a moderately Orthodox Jewish home; we were a very happy and loving family. I was the middle child of three with an older brother Ben and a younger sister, Lusia. We also had relatives in Piotrkow, including three cousins and lots of friends. I look back on it as a happy childhood.

I started school a year early, at the age of six. I was very good at Polish but not great at maths. When I finished the third year and was about to start the new term in September, when I was nearly nine years old, everything changed. Germany declared war on the first of September 1939, and the next day bombs were falling on my home town.

By nightfall families were fleeing east, our family among them. By early morning we had reached Sulejow, a small town some fifteen kilometres away, where my parents decided to stop, as my father had met his younger brother, Fishel, his wife, Irene, and their two-year-old daughter, Hania. But later that day the bombing started there too, and within minutes much of the town was in flames.

We, together with other families, were in one of the few brick buildings in the town, and it was only my mother's presence of mind that saved us. She stood at the door and prevented us from fleeing the safety of the house. When the bombing seemed to have stopped, she opened the door and we all ran to the nearby woods. We were lucky to survive that short, but perilous run, as German planes were strafing over our heads. For the next few days we travelled by night and hid in the forest by day to avoid the bombing. When my parents decided to return home, we thought the whole town *was on fire. Later we found out that some coal trucks on the railway had received a direct hit.*

Poland was invaded in two weeks. Everything changed.

Our town was the first one in the whole of Poland to have a ghetto – an area where all the Jews were sent to live. It was in an old, rundown part of town. By the 1ˢᵗ of November 1939, we were removed from our homes and incarcerated in the ghetto. My father managed to find two rooms and a kitchen, with toilet but no bathroom. We were lucky to have this accommodation for our family of five, and at some point we even shared it with my mother's sister Gucia, who came to join us from Sieradz. As the ghetto became more and more crowded we had to give up one room to another family, but we were still lucky to have a large room and a kitchen to ourselves. As large areas of Poland on the German border were annexed and became part of Germany, Jews were driven out and many of them made their way to the Piotrkow Ghetto. The original number of people in the ghetto was 15,000, the Jewish population of Piotrkow, which grew to 28,000. There were now as many as two or three families to a room, and the inadequate sanitary conditions caused a lot of epidemics, which reduced the numbers to 24,000.

People over the age of twelve had to wear a white armband with a blue star of David, and anyone found without it could be shot. That didn't apply to me as I was too young. We had curfews and we were deprived of the most basic human rights. There was a shortage of food, but the Jewish Administration which was set up tried to help people; there were soup kitchens and other provisions for the very poor. The ghetto was also patrolled by German soldiers with their rifles and revolvers.

There were also large notices plastered on walls asking us to give anything of value by bringing things to a specific address on a certain date. Men of working age were used for labour in various places. They would leave the ghetto in a column and march under German guard to the place of work and return in the evening, always heavily guarded. There were also people being shot for no reason at all, and the Germans were making all sorts of demands via the Jewish administration, some of which could not possibly be met. There was a particular German officer who used to turn up with a big black ferocious dog and set him on people.

In 1942, rumours began to circulate that the ghetto was to be reduced to just the Jewish administration and those with work permits. The majority of the inhabitants were to be rounded up, selections would take place, and people would be deported to death camps like Treblinka, Majdanek or Sobibor. These were dreaded camps. The atmosphere became very tense and people were in a state of panic trying to find ways to save themselves. Those who could arranged to go into hiding outside the ghetto. This required not only the means to pay but also connections and trusted friends outside, for if you were caught or betrayed, the penalty was certain death.

Although my father knew a lot of people outside the ghetto, he was actually introduced, together with my uncle Joseph Klein, to a Christian man of German origin from Czestochowa, who was willing to hide two Jewish girls for the duration of the deportations and then to return them to their parents. This man was highly recommended, and my parents together with my aunt and uncle, the Kleins, struck the deal. The man was paid in advance and he said that he will come for me the following week and return for Idzia the week after.

The journey, by train, was very scary and we were very frightened. There was actually a reward for handing in Jews and if someone looked at us for more than a few seconds we thought they were suspecting us of being Jewish. We travelled on false papers. The train would stop occasionally, German soldiers would get on and search people and look at travel documents. It was terrifying.

We finally arrived and found ourselves in a house on the outskirts of Czestochowa with the man's parents-in-law. They were not exactly pleased to have us but they tolerated us and didn't ill-treat us. Life was very precarious and we were extremely vulnerable. We were frightened and homesick and exposed to many dangers.

To make our identity more anonymous, we were supposed to be relatives from Warsaw. However, we were not very well briefed and when asked questions by visitors – like the actual relationship or our exact address — we were often stumped for answers and had to do some quick thinking.

Whenever there was a knock on the door, we were quickly bundled into a wardrobe and had to stay there till the visitors left, but occasionally it was OK for us to mix.

We both missed our parents, but Idzia was so homesick that she asked to go back home. She was told that it was not yet safe as the deportations were still happening. But when she told the family that she could go to very good friends, the ones in Piotrkow who were looking after valuables for her parents, they agreed.

I thought that Idzia was lucky because she was back with her parents, and I still had to wait for what seemed like a lifetime. When I was eventually taken back and handed over to my father, Idzia's father was present too. He turned white with shock and asked, "Where is my daughter? What have you done with my child?" He was told that she had been left some time previously with their good friends. I still remember vividly my uncle with his hands behind his back looking down at the floor, pacing there and back, repeating, "What have you done with my child?" I was shocked beyond words. We just looked on helplessly.

Many years later I learned that the man had gone to these friends, collected a suitcase full of valuables and then departed with Idzia and the suitcase. Idzia was never seen again, and the circumstances of her disappearance remain a mystery to this day. Her mother, Dora Klein, the only survivor of that family, never got over it, and whenever we met we couldn't bear to talk about it. Not knowing what happened is so painful because the imagination goes wild and my aunt lived with that pain till the end of her life.

CHAPTER FORTY-FOUR
MALA'S TESTIMONY

Back in the ghetto, my family were reunited, my brother had a work permit, my father, mother and Lusia were all in hiding during the deportations, each one with a different family. But we were in terrible danger. Our home was now a corner of a room in the small ghetto, two half streets housing 2,400 people, the remainder of the 24,000.

When people thought it was safe they had started returning to the ghetto, and the authorities turned a blind eye. Anybody in the ghetto without a work permit was "an illegal", but nevertheless it was informally declared that the "illegals" were safe. This prompted those still in hiding to surface, but they were walking into a trap.

Over the next few days they rounded up most of the "illegals" and took them to the Great Synagogue, once a beautiful building. They were kept there without sanitation, light, heat, food or water. To amuse themselves, the Ukrainian Guards would shoot into the synagogue through the windows, killing and wounding people. Tragically my mother and Lusia were among the people taken to the synagogue. The only reason I was saved is that when they stormed into our crowded room I was in bed, and my mother said to the policeman in charge that I wasn't well and he said that I could stay behind. As they were being led out I closed my eyes tightly and cried till my father returned from work.

I never saw my mother or sister again. On the 20th of December 1942, they were taken out of the synagogue at dawn and marched to the Rakow Forest in groups of fifty where newly dug mass graves awaited them. They were told to undress and stand at the edge of the graves and they were shot. Those only wounded were buried with the dead. My mother was thirty-seven and Lusia was eight years old.

There were now three of us left, my father, Ben and me. It was heart-breaking.

My aunt Irene, whose husband had been shot with others at the Jewish cemetery, was rounded up and taken away screaming, "Who will look after my child?" By then I was the only female member of the Helfgott family left, Hania was five years old and I was twelve. I took care of her.

We were still living in that corner of the room, in the small ghetto referred to also as the Block. Ben was working in a glass factory called Hortensja and my father was working too. But as children, we were considered of no use and we were "illegal" anyway.

So there were now just two groups of workers left, Hortensja and Dietrich und Fischer a plywood manufacturer at Bugaj, and when the ghetto was about to be liquidated they searched for all the remaining illegals and lined us up in a column outside the ghetto gates for deportation. We were surrounded by police and soldiers with rifles at the ready. We were all panic stricken, babies were crying, mothers were frightened and distressed, organized in lines ready to board the lorries to take us away. The woman in front of us, with a baby in her arms, was hit over the head with a gun, blood was pouring from her head and the baby was screaming. She was in a terrible state; it was a shocking sight to witness.

I don't know what possessed me, but I spotted an SS officer, not far from me on my right, and I went up to him and said that I have been separated from my father and brother, they are inside the ghetto, may I go back to them? He looked very surprised, a little bemused; I still remember his face, perhaps he had a twelve-year-old daughter at home. He called over a policeman and ordered him to take me back to the ghetto. On the way I said, "Just a minute, I have to collect my cousin." The policeman said that permission was only for me, my cousin would not be allowed to return. It was an impossible situation; I was terrified by the choice of leaving Hania or losing the chance of being reunited with my father and Ben. I begged and pleaded, I kept on arguing, saying that I could not go back to the ghetto without her, and he eventually relented and allowed Hania to go with me. "Take her quickly," he said.

At this point I must stress that the Holocaust was full of such dilemmas; there were so many heart-wrenching cases.

So, there were still four of us, but we were no longer a family. We were lucky to be allocated to Bugaj together with my father and Ben, but men and women were always housed separately in camps. So their barracks were situated at one end of this huge complex and ours at the other end, but we managed to see one another. Here I too became a slave labourer. We worked long hours and Hania, who was very attached to me, didn't like me to leave her, but she had no choice and since we worked shifts there were always some women around who would keep an eye on her.

The plywood was manufactured there, quite an interesting process, and from it we produced round wooden huts in sections which were packaged and sent to the German soldiers at the front.

My friend Pema Blachman was there with her parents and sister, and because her father had a position on the "council" they enjoyed the privilege of a tiny hut all to themselves, which I thought was the ultimate in luxury. I was in a large barrack, sharing a bottom bunk with Hania Pema's mother, who had the book Gone with the Wind, and since children were not allowed to read books meant for adults, Pema used to read it secretly when her mother was out and relate it to me on our secret walks. Meeting a friend outside working hours was no simple matter because Hania would not let me out of her sight, she was so afraid of losing me.

Towards the end of 1944, we were all marched to the railway station. Ben and my father were sent to Buchenwald concentration camp, and Hania and I, after a four-and-a-half hour horrendous journey in cattle trucks without any food or water, ended up in Ravensbruck concentration camp.

On arrival we queued at a reception centre where all our personal details were recorded; not surprising, knowing how meticulous the Germans were at record keeping. Our few possessions were taken from us, we were told to strip, our heads were shaved, we went through colds communal showers and when we emerged at the other end, we were given the standard striped concentration camp: pyjama-like garb, and clogs. When we looked at one another we could not *recognize each other. It was a shock to the system. By then we had been going through this war for over five years, and each time we arrived at a new place we would say, "It can't get worse than this!"*

Now we felt that we had been really stripped of our identity and personality, and our very souls as well; we all looked alike, we could not even recognize one another. We began to lose hope, and without hope there is no survival. Depression and despair were setting in, and the years of suffering, deprivation and the deteriorating conditions started to take their toll. My aunt Frania Klein died soon after arrival, and a few days later so did my friend Pema Blachman. Hania was getting thinner and my main worry was how to keep her alive.

We had daily roll calls, which meant that we had to rise at five a.m. and stand outside the barracks, by six. It was terribly stressful to wash and get ready in time. Sometimes they counted us again and again, and we had to stand for hours. It was in the depths of a European winter, and we were wearing thin clothing with no underwear, no tights and no outer garments. People used to faint or die.

Our rations were a slice of black bread and soup which resembled dishwater, but we were glad to have it, and a cup of imitation coffee which was really brown water. Sometimes we would also get a knob of margarine. We were in the women's camp, where some of the women worked outside in the fields, but neither Hania nor I worked. Occasionally one of the women would smuggle in a potato, turnip or radish, but if anyone were caught the punishment was very severe, usually death. On one occasion my aunt Dora brought me a turnip.

We didn't know it but the Russian army was approaching and the war was drawing to an end. Once again we had to climb into cattle trucks, and after a shorter journey we found ourselves in Bergen-Belsen. When the train stopped we could hear dogs barking, the soldiers shouting, "Raus, schnell!" We formed ourselves into a column and marched to the camp. When we arrived there was no room for us and they put us up in a tent outside overnight. There were hundreds of people there speaking all different languages; it was quite chaotic.

The following morning we entered the camp and

what we saw defies description. The first thing that hit you was the smog and smell; there were people, but they looked like skeletons and shuffled along like zombies. You could be speaking to someone and they would just collapse and die in front of you. There were dead bodies everywhere and piles of naked, twisted, decaying corpses. The sanitation was in the form of open pits. Typhus was rife and there was an air of utter hopelessness. The degradation, humiliation and despair were clearly visible on people's faces. The barracks were so overcrowded that one that should have held eighty to one hundred people would have hundreds.

Again, I was lucky. I had heard there was a children's barracks somewhere in the camp and set out to find it. We were interviewed by Dr Bimko and Sister Luba who were in charge. After asking a lot of questions they said I was too old at fourteen, but they agreed to take Hania. However, she was adamant she would not stay without me, so I said I would try to persuade her and bring her back tomorrow. There was no way Hania would leave me and they decided to take us both in.

That was an unimaginable stroke of luck; we would not have survived in the main camp. Anne Frank was in Bergen-Belsen at the time but she died in March.

The children here were mostly Dutch with a very special history of their own, and it was run by Jewish women whom we called sisters – nursing sisters – and they were kind and loving and did everything they could to find us food. When they went to the kitchens for soup they would beg for a little extra for the children.

Even in this marginally better environment I still succumbed to typhus, and I remember lying on my bunk by the window barely conscious when I saw people running. I didn't know where or why they were running, all I could think of was – how did they have the strength to run? I couldn't move a muscle.

That was the moment of liberation, on 15th April 1945 when the British troops entered the camp. Under the supervision of Brigadier Glyn Hughes, a hospital was set up, and thanks to the expertise of the medical and relief teams I and many others were nursed back to health. I still remember their dedication and kindness after suffering years of cruelty and deprivation.

I am often asked whether it is easy for me to speak about these painful experiences, and the answer is no – I relive them every time. So you may well ask, why do I do it? Well … I had the good luck to survive, so I feel it is my duty to tell what happened in those dark days in Europe. I speak for all those people whose voices were silenced, many generations wiped out, and there is no one to remember them and if we don't it will be as if they have never existed.

There is a lesson to be learned from the Holocaust. It demonstrates what can happen when a despot rules and civilization breaks down, and when there is prejudice, hate and discrimination.

As we look around the world and continue to see so many examples of man's inhumanity to man, there is something we should always have in mind – be vigilant, stand up and be counted, don't be a bystander.

CHAPTER FORTY-FIVE

EVIE

All the way home I am thinking furiously. About Mala, and everything she went through. How she had the incredible strength to carry on after the war – making a new life in Sweden with Hania, until she heard that her brother, Ben, was alive and living in England and they were reunited.

How she married an architect and had children, and did a degree in sociology. And now she speaks to thousands of people every year about her experiences.

How brave Mala was, and is. How, after everything she went through, she could have decided that being Jewish was too dangerous and difficult. That she should concentrate on fitting in. But she'd had her identity taken away from her once already. And she wasn't going to lose it again. I wonder if I'd have her strength to carry on with life after everything she'd gone through. After hearing her story I appreciate everything I have so much more now. My sister and my parents, our nice house and having food in the fridge and the central heating. Our freedom, even going to school … just everything.

I reach out and hold Lottie's hand, and she squeezes it back. I think how amazing it was that we both worried about each other on the day of the attack. Was it twin intuition? I don't think it was. It's just natural to worry about someone you love when something dangerous is happening.

"I am never going to complain about anything ever again," I say, which makes Mum and Dad laugh, a nice, warm laugh.

I am Jewish, I realize. It's nothing to do with the religious thing that Lottie seems to like, and it's not about Jewish law, or politics or anything.

It's just that there need to be as many people as possible telling the truth about what happened in the Holocaust, and before that and more than that – what is happening now. If I dodge that on some technicality – because I don't feel it enough – then I am letting Mala down. Not just her, all the millions of people who were killed, people who don't get to speak for themselves.

And then there's the people who could be killed for being Jewish in the future. Or not even for being Jewish. Just for being different.

Be vigilant. Stand up and be counted. Don't be a bystander. That's what Mala said.

I let go of Lottie's hand and I get out my phone and I text Amina. *TikTok project is go*, I write. *Let's start tomorrow.*

It's time to start living again.

CHAPTER FORTY-SIX

LOTTIE

The crowd is buzzing, lively, unpredictable. I'm worried about Evie. Is she really up to appearing on stage yet? Is this the right competition for her?

"She'll be fine!" says Mum, when I say this to her.

"It's the Jewish Teenage Stand-Up of the Year. It's not like her school."

"Don't worry, Lottie," says Dad. "They'll like a new face. And after what Evie's been through, this'll be easy. Nothing much scares her now."

Evie always was brave, I think. I was the

worrier. But now I'm a lot braver. And Evie admits she has fears too.

"And anyway," says Mum, "Evie's got her own supporters. Look. She's got us, and Amina's with her backstage, and there's Noah and his parents and grandma, and Hannah and her family..."

"And Benny," I say, because Evie seems to be getting quite friendly with him.

"Oooh," says Mum, sitting up straight. "Is he here? Maybe Evie will introduce me?"

"Give her some space, Mum," I say, and she grins back and says, "Of course!"

Then the lights dim and we're all shouting and cheering as Evie comes on stage.

My sister. Looking really sharp in a black leather mini dress, a black top, a shimmering red scarf and make-up, as applied by Amina. Noah, on my left side, is standing up and clapping. We're not the only ones making some noise. Although the press never named Evie, word spread that one of Bex Harris's daughters had been injured. I know, because about a million people asked me about it at Hannah's synagogue, which has now pretty much become my synagogue. As Mum is a hero now in the Jewish community for speaking out against antisemitism, Evie and I are off to a good start too. Plus she's got a whole new audience on TikTok.

And she's off.

"Well, hey guys," she says, "how are you? Everyone good? Everyone safe? That's excellent. I have to tell you, I like things to be safe. Like, mega safe. Like, if I had my way there's be a knife arch at the door, and you'd all be vetted by MI5. I mean there's nothing that says a fun night out like compulsory pat down for all, is there?

"Anyway, got some advice for you all if you find yourself in a tricky situation. Forget self-defence classes … get yourself a bin handler." Laughter, a great burst of it. "Yup, a wheelie bin is your best line of defence when a homicidal maniac is running towards you. Just reach in and find some used nappies to throw at him. Shove the wheelie bin right at him. It'll ruin your nails. But you know, kind of worth it."

She's on great form and the crowd love it. "I

have to admit, I'm pretty new to being Jewish. I'm still working out what it really means. It's odd, isn't it? It's a religion, but you can be totally unreligious and still be Jewish. And Jews all look different, and come from all countries in the world … except maybe North Korea … and speak lots of different languages and have different politics, and there are loads of famous Jewish people – like Drake … and Einstein … and Ross and Monica on *Friends*… And they don't really have anything in common at all, except some people think they want to take over the world. Which is weird really. Because Drake and Monica and Einstein… I mean, it'd probably be fun if they ruled the world, but I can't see them working together very well. Drake would sing, and Einstein would have to do all the clever stuff, and Monica would make all the food, and you know – be anxious. Because it's a fact that all Jewish women in films and books have to be bossy, anxious and spoiled.

"I suppose I am a little spoiled too. I have my very own Uber driver. It's so convenient. Much better than when Dad had a boring office job."

I glance to the side to see if Dad minds this dig, but it's OK, he's laughing along with everyone else. He's been in a good mood ever since his agent said he loved the new script and has sent it to production companies.

"Anyway, seems to me that comedy is really important to Jewish people. We've had so many bad things happen to us that we need to laugh more than the average person. And we need to celebrate. So here are a few things I love about being Jewish.

"There's the food. Which other religion has a festival which is celebrated with fried potatoes and doughnuts? Awesome, right? It almost makes up for Pesach – Passover – when it's all eggs and cardboard.

"And then there's the Yiddish language. It has the best words. My favourite one is 'zaftig', which means 'pleasingly plump'. Isn't that the coolest concept ever? Isn't that what the world needs? When I'm rich and famous and people are begging me to set up my own fashion label, guess what I'm going to call it? You got it. Ms Zaftig."

She does a twirl. "I might even change my name. Evie Zaftig. What do you think?"

She's shining tonight, my sister. She's making everyone laugh, and at the same time I can see Mum and Dad's eyes shining with tears, because she was in such danger, and now she's strong and funny and surviving.

"Before I go, I'm going to shout out to two people. First my twin sister Lottie. Now, just in case you're looking for another zaftig beauty in the audience, don't bother, because we're the world's least identical twins. Poor Lottie is cursed with being tall and elegant and slim ... with none of my zaftig curves, I mean, how does she cope...? And she's much more of a serious Jew than I am as well; she's learning Hebrew and she's going to shul. Everyone should have a twin like her. And if you're not lucky enough to have a twin, then you need an amazing friend. My friend Amina is here, and she's going to come out and do this last bit with me."

Amina steps out on to the stage. I'm surprised to see that she's wearing a hijab, which she doesn't usually. But then I suppose that's what comedy is – an exaggerated version of life, which you can laugh at sometimes. It's not a bad coping mechanism.

Evie and Amina are doing a rap – "We're here to tell you 'bout an ancient rift / It's gone on for years, so we won't be swift" – and everyone's filming them on their phones, and laughing and cheering.

I hear it, then. The faint sound of a siren outside. Panic sweeps over me. I feel for the inhaler in my pocket. It's there. And the siren fades away, and nothing happens. We're safe.

Hannah whispers, "She's amazing!"

"I know," I say, watching as Amina and Evie take a bow and the clapping goes on and on and on.

"Are you OK?" asks Hannah. She always knows.

"Yeah, I just heard the siren, and felt a bit scared."

"Me too," says Hannah, and she reaches out and squeezes my arm, and I know that even if I do feel scared I'm never going to be alone with that.

After the competition, we go out to celebrate Evie coming second. We order pizzas and Dad fills up our glasses: wine for the adults, Coke for us.

He raises his glass in the air. "Ladies and gentlemen, let's drink to Evie. Cheers!"

But before we can drink, Mum interrupts. "No," she says, "this time let's make it a real Jewish toast, for a Jewish competition." She raises her glass. "*L'chaim*! To life!"

As we echo her, *To life!* my eyes meet Evie's. We grin at each other. Because this is it. The way to deal with the stuff that scares us.

We celebrate the good times.

We seize opportunities.

We laugh, we cry, we feel every moment.

We live our lives. We love our lives. We love life itself.

This is what we're here for.

L'chaim!

ACKNOWLEDGEMENTS

First, infinite gratitude and love to Mala Tribich, for agreeing to help with this book. We spent hours together, and it was a life-changing experience for me – one which opened my eyes to the depth of suffering that you endured, but also the spirit of survival and love of life that is so important. "Do not be a bystander" is your message, and I will try and live up to that.

Thank you as well to Michelle Hyer of JW3, who introduced me to Mala.

Thank you to Ann and Bob Kirk, whose lives

as Kindertransport refugees are adapted in this book. Your story was moving and inspiring, and I feel so lucky to have met you. Thank you to Kathrin Pieren and to Abigail Morris at the Jewish Museum in Camden for our conversations about various exhibitions there.

Thank you to my agent Jenny Savill, who gently persuaded me that I could write this book, and to all at Scholastic for your support and immense patience while I wrestled with it for far too long: thank you Samantha Selby Smith, Miriam Farbey, Lauren Fortune, Gen Herr, Peter Matthews and Rachel Phillipps. And thank you to Liam Drane for a great cover.

I could not have written it without my colleagues at the *Jewish Chronicle*. Having a job which allows me to think and talk about Jewish stuff all the time was extremely helpful! Especial thanks to Stephen Pollard.

Thank you to Hilary, my childhood friend, whose journey to Judaism has been absolutely joyful and fascinating and has made me think so much. And thank you to Jesse for much deep discussion of life as a Jewish woman.

Thank you to all my friends, for support and questions and advice, and reading. You know who you are!

Rabbi Laura Janner Klausner oversaw one d'var Torah in this book and Rabbi David Mason another. And for additional support and insights, Rabbi Boruch Altein, Rabbi Yakov Tatz and Rabbi Herschel Gluck, all very much appreciated.

Two books which helped me write this one were both written by Dvora Baum: *Feeling Jewish (A Book for Just About Anyone)* and *The Jewish Joke: An Essay with Examples*. And I also loved talking to comedians Josh Howie and Rachel Creeger about Jewish stand-up. I have read many books and articles on contemporary antisemitism, too many to list, but especial thanks to David Hirsh, David Aaronovitch and Jonathan Freedland.

Thank you to my family; Laurence, Phoebe and Judah; Mum and Dad; Alun, Deborah and Jeremy, Joshua and Rebecca, Avital and Eliana. And to my aunts, uncles and cousins – between us, we represent so many different ways of being Jewish.

This book is dedicated to the victims of antisemitism, especially my great-grandfather, Abraham Buznic, of blessed memory, murdered at Auschwitz alongside his family and countless others.

ABOUT THE AUTHOR

Growing up as a voracious reader in Hertfordshire, Keren David had two ambitions: to write a book and to live in London. Several decades on, she has achieved both. She was distracted by journalism, starting out at eighteen as a messenger girl, then working as a reporter, news editor, features editor and feature writer for national newspapers and magazines, she's currently associate editor at the *Jewish Chronicle*. She has lived in Glasgow and Amsterdam, where in eight years she learned enough Dutch to order coffee and buy fruit and vegetables. She returned to London in 2007 with her husband and two children, and started writing YA books, *What We're Scared Of* is her twelfth. She has two black cats, Wilbur and Dexter who used to live next door but adopted her family when their owner moved to a cat-free flat.